THE FIRST LADY

A NOVEL

BY

WILLIAM HELLINGER

© *2004 WILLIAM HELLINGER.*
All Rights Reserved.

No part of this book may be reproduced, stored in a retrieval system, or transmitted by any means without the written permission of the author.

First published by 1st Books 11/01/2004

ISBN: 1-4140-3829-1 (e)
ISBN: 1-4140-3827-5 (sc)
ISBN: 1-4140-3828-3 (dj)

Printed in the United States of America
Bloomington, Indiana

This book is printed on acid-free paper.

Cover Painting by: Lorna Greene

NOVEL EDITED BY:

ROBERT RIND

DEDICATED TO MY WIFE LORNA GREENE, ARTIST, WHO PUSHED THE HELL OUT OF ME TO FINISH THE NOVEL.

Table of Contents

Chapter One   Belair Services Rendered 1

Chapter Two   Aunt Bea's House 13

Chapter Three   Saturday Night Arrives................................... 19

Chapter Four   Revelation & Seduction.................................... 33

Chapter Five   Robert Has Disappeared 47

Chapter Six   Missing Person's The Investigation 53

Chapter Seven   Detective Milano's Report............................... 61

Chapter Eight   Harut City, Bokuf Eight months later 65

Chapter Nine   Hope is a Woman 81

Chapter Ten   A New Life For Roberta 85

Chapter Eleven   Shipping Out.. 95

Chapter Twelve   Free At Last 99

Chapter Thirteen   A Mother's Help 105

Chapter Fourteen   In The Nick Of Time................................... 113

Chapter Fifteen   The Assault 119

Chapter Sixteen   Paris City of Hope.. 129

Chapter Seventeen   To Be or Not To Be 137

Chapter Eighteen   To Live or Die in Paris............................... 147

Chapter Nineteen   The Sheik's Hit Men 159

Chapter Twenty   A Star is Born 163

Chapter Twenty-One   Home Again... 171

Chapter Twenty-Two   Roberta Mann Movie Star.................... 177

Chapter Twenty-Three   The Sheik Abdicates 189

Chapter Twenty-Four   The Escape... 193

Chapter Twenty-Five   Mr. & Mrs. Candidate........................... 199

Chapter Twenty-Six A First Lady At Last 201
Chapter Twenty-Seven A Night to Remember........................... 205

Chapter One
Belair Services Rendered

A gust of the summer wind bursts through the open window and its current of air parts the silk drapes allowing a shaft of light into the dimly lit room capturing two sweating naked bodies in an intercourse of sexual joy, on an extra large king size bed.

The female's soft quivering voice moans of ecstasy that increases in intensity as her male lover increases his thrust into her "opening of joy."

On top is the lean, athletic built body of Robert Anthony, a 24 year old, handsome All-American type, with a neck length Titian red hair pony tail.

The tall shapely female body underneath Robert is that of Diana Stuart, a beautiful honey blond ex-model in her late thirties, who is now sinking her finger nails into Robert's back as he moans and groans to Diana's screams of orgasmic splendor "Ohhh. I'm coming Robert. I'm coming don't stop."

With that outburst, Robert pushes his loins deeper into Diana as she continues her cries of ecstasy and screams "Oh, my God Robert."

For several moments the passionate couple stay attached, when Robert looks down at Diana's face and sees that she is happy and extremely contented. Robert kisses her tenderly before lifting himself off her body, "God, it is true. You are the best," says Diana while sighing softly.

Robert laughs jokingly and tells Diana, "I bet you say that to all of your lovers."

Annoyed by Robert's remark Diana replies, "No. Not unless I mean it." Turning to the lamp on the night table she snaps her fingers and the lamp is turned on, but the light is just a little too bright, so another snap of her fingers and the light dims down. Diana picks up her robe from the floor, puts it on, then sits at the edge of the bed. She turns to Robert, stares directly into his baby blue eyes and with sincere honesty declares, "Robert I want you to know I'm not one of those Hollywood wives who just go to bed with anyone. I never did until I caught Harry with an actress. She was starring in one of the pictures he was producing. I Caught them right here in this bed. So now I do to my dear husband just what he does to me." Robert trying to lighten up the moment asks, "Is it anyone I might know?"

"Probably," Diana responds smiling.

Robert sensing that Diana is a little set back reassures her with, "Look, I really don't care who she is and I do understand your want for revenge."

Diana gazes at Robert for a moment, then her lips form a broad smile and she tells him, "You are here only
because you were highly recommended by my dear friend Kate."

Robert responds to Diana with respect and understanding, "Kate had a similar Hollywood story. She is a very sweet nice lady just like you."

Diana appreciates Robert's concern and candor about Hollywood's neglected wives and how love starved these women are. She wraps her arms around his neck and plants a long, wet hot kiss on his sensual lips. When her kiss is finally concluded Diana whispers, "You're very nice, Robert. Your lips are very soft and your breath is very sweet." She lays her head down on the pillow next to him, closes her eyes and a soft smile of contentment forms over her lovely face.

Robert lying there with a smile of sexual contentment slowly closes his eyes and his mind starts to ponder his situation. Here he is again, screwing another Producers unhappy wife to get a part in a movie. But so far all he's gotten from any of them was a measly three line part, extra work and lots of work and lots of promises. It's great for him to get laid, but what he needs, and what he wants most of all is that big part in a picture to show off his acting talents. Then he thinks, "What if I never get that chance then what?"

His thoughts now go to alternate careers if in the event he doesn't get that acting break. Thinking about it, he says to himself, "maybe I'll become a cop with the LA Police Department or even a fireman with their Fire Department. But, then again while they can be secure, exciting jobs, there is a risk of danger."

He then likes the idea of maybe becoming a teacher of drama in the high school system. Realization then comes to his mind as to the way the public school system has changed because of drugs, gangs and the wildness of the youths of today. It can be dangerous, a possible Blackboard Jungle situation.

He now thinks that acting is his destiny and he should stick to it till the bitter end. So from here on, he will make sure that he confirms all of his deals before he barters away his services.

Robert's thoughts then turned to his mother and father, parents he never knew. They were killed in a cross walk on Ventura Boulevard by a drunken driver when Robert was six months old. His mother was wheeling him in a stroller across the four lane street when a car bore down on them. If it hadn't been for his father pushing his carriage out of harms-way he wouldn't be here today having problems trying to get acting jobs by servicing those lonely neglected producers' wives as he laughs at himself.

All of Robert's fond recollections were of his Aunt Bea, his mother's older sister as his only parent that he loves and adores. She had raised him and taught him all the things he needed to know, all that was right and wrong. But life is a bitch and he blamed himself for his short comings.

Robert turned onto his side to look at Diana. He stares at her for a moment and then boldly and plainly states, "Of course, Kate told you I'm an actor looking for work."

Diana rolls her beautiful round eyes wide open smiles and says, "Yes, she did tell me that and I do understand where you're coming from. Listen, my husband is getting ready to do a movie in Montana and I read the script. You'd be right for a couple of parts, damn good ones, too. Robert, I promise I will make sure that he casts you in one of those roles."

It sounds great but Robert has heard this dialogue before. "Are you sure your husband will listen to your recommendation?" asks Robert pointedly.

Diana's smile turns into a sober look. She replies firmly, "Harry has to. I've got him by the balls and money bags."

Robert is extremely impressed by Diana's black-mailing heart. "You won't be sorry. I'm a hell of an actor."

Diana looks at him for a moment then blurts out, "If you can act the way you fuck, you'll probably win an academy award." Diana's funny sage remark made them both bust out in laughter and roll around in bed playfully

When Diana catches her breath an inquisitive look comes over her face, "Robert, Kate never told me how you two got together," asks Diana.

"Oh, she didn't? Well, I met Kate through another woman who had the same problem," admits a surprised Robert.

"Do I know this lady?" Diana probes.

"Probably," retorts Robert laughing.

"Now you're teasing me," declares Diana in a child-like voice.

"Oh, I wouldn't do that to you, Diana," says Robert jokingly. Then Robert explains. "Diana, seriously, you might know who she is so I can't give you her name. If anyone asked me about you, I would also protect you."

"Thank you Robert, you are a gentleman. That's one of the reasons why Kate recommended you," says Diana gratefully.

Robert acknowledged Diana's compliment with a shy grin.

Diana's lips formed a sensual smile. She gently placed the palm of her hand on Robert's bare chest and slowly glided it from pectoral to pectoral.

Diana sees that Robert likes what she is doing, but still probing she curiously states, "Robert, you must be very busy servicing other ladies in this town."

He is annoyed at what Diana has said. He pushes her hand away from his chest and gruffly says, "No Diana, I'm not a Hollywood stud. I only sell myself hoping this will lead to my big break in films."

Diana is a little sorry and embarrassed for her previous remark and says to him. "I understand, Robert."

"I hope you do Diana," he replies and then laughs ironically and tells Diana. "You know, I always thought it was so easy that talent was all you needed to get ahead, but talent is not enough, is it Diana?"

"It's a tough business Robert and a dirty one. I know what I'm talking about," Diana answers.

"Yeah, that's why you've got to know the right people," Robert laments.

"You're absolutely right, Robert. You've got to know the right people who can help you. That's the key to success," agrees Diana with a strong confirmation.

"You know, I met this lady at Mahoganys' where I was working and she's the one who set me straight. I used to be naive". Diana interrupts Robert. "You work at Mahoganys on the Sunset strip?" asks Diana who reacts very surprised. Robert nods his head. Isn't that the club where male dancers perform nude for women?" continues Diana.

WILLIAM HELLINGER

Robert laughs, "Yes, I'm one of those strippers, but not nude. We only strip down to our bikini jock straps. I work there four nights a week." Robert wanted to tell Diana the reason why he was working at Mahoganys'. He didn't think she would care but perhaps, maybe she might have. Any way it was really none of her think she would care but perhaps, maybe she might have. Any way it was really none of her business, just his.

Robert's mind races back, remembering why he was working at Mahoganys'. He needed to make a lot of money real quick. He had found out that his Aunt Bea had run out of her savings because of having spent most of her money to raise him and now she needed more money to send him to college at U.S.C. She took a mortgage out on the house, a $100,000 loan. She used that money for Robert's education, mortgage payments and the rest of the money for them to live on.

Now, that money was running out and his aunt was almost flat broke. His full time night job, earning $240 a week at Blockmasters movie rentals, wasn't quite enough. They just about managed. Robert had hoped he would make some extra money from acting jobs to fill the money gap, but movie work was far and in between.

Things were looking bleak, when one night one of his steady customers, a sexy forty year old lady came in to rent some movies. She liked Robert and she knew he wasn't making much money at Blockmasters while having hopes for a break as an actor. She asked Robert if he wanted to make a hell of a lot more money working part time at night. More money in a week than he could ever make working at Blockbmasters for a month.

Robert's prayers were answered. He could have shouted Hallelujah. Of course he was interested, he told the good lady. But before he committed himself he wanted to know what kind of job it was and the sexy woman answered "Dancing at Mahoganys'." She told him she was one of the managers at the club and they had lost one of their dancers to a female customer who married him. His wife now didn't want him to continue prancing himself in front of other sex starved women. These women make a play for every dancer at the club, so the spot had to be filled as soon as possible. Robert was the perfect type she said and if he wanted the job, it was his. Robert laughed and told the sexy lady that he's a very good dancer, but didn't think he could do the kind of dancing that was required at Mahoganys'.

THE FIRST LADY

The lady liking Robert for his honesty gave him a sexy smile and told him not to be concerned about that because she would help him. She knew that the club's female audience would flip over him. Mahoganys' sexy lady manager taught him how to swing his hips and the other vital parts of his body that women just go crazy over. It was easy for Robert, he was an actor and actors are quick to learn.

Aunt Bea believed that Robert was still working at the movie rental store and was very happy with the extra money Robert gave her. She thanks God that Blockmasters appreciated her nephew. Robert knows he could stay at Mahoganys' for as long they wanted him, or until he gets his movie break.

Robert's mind zips back to Diana and he asks her, "Have you ever been to Mahoganys'?" "No, but some of my Beverly Hills lady friends have," confesses Diana. "You might have met them there." Diana then scans Robert's naked body and giggles, "I can just hear those blasé, sex starved women yelling and screaming. Take it off. Take it off. Take it all off." Diana's mimicking the women, makes Robert's thoughts regress to that night at Mahoganys' when he met Marian Crosby. That night was just like any other night, the club was loaded with women of every age, shape and color.

He was on stage dancing his ass off. A spot light was on him and every time he bumped he would grind his hips, the ladies laughed, screamed and yelled for him to take off his clothes. Some women even encouraged him to disrobe more quickly by tipping him, by placing money into his pockets. He was sweating his balls off. He danced down to his "G" string. Some women cried with passion, while other women tried grabbing every part of his naked anatomy. He was amazed by the way the women in the room reacted. Every time he took a piece of his clothes off, they became crazed, uninhibited unashamed just like a bunch of men at a stag party, except for one woman.

An attractive brunette in her forties, with a nice Figure, sitting at a table near the stage all by herself. He had observed the lady during his performance just staring at him, smiling and sipping her glass of wine. Just before he was about to end his performance, the lady vaulted up from her chair, gave him a sexy smile and slip a roll of money into his "G" string. He smiled at her nodding his head in thanks. When he ended his performance

7

the women applauded, screamed and whistled their appreciation as he left the stage, bowing to his grateful audience.

He was tired and sweaty when he got back to the dressing room that he shared with the other dancers. He dumped all of his tips onto his dressing table and when he counted the money, he was surprised. It was a bonanza, $400. The best tips, he had ever had, at Mahoganys' for one night of work. He and the other dancers usually averaged about $250 a night which was great money for them.

As he was about to leave the dressing room for home he noticed a roll of money against his tissue box. He discovered that it was a $100 bill with a note rolled up with it. The note read, "Robert, I think you are great. I would love to meet you." It was signed Marian Crosby, 555-2465.

Robert called Marian Crosby the next day. Excited to hear from him she took him to lunch at the Palms in West Hollywood. She was a sweet lady and he liked the way she smelled. He was a little red faced when she told him that he was a great dancer, very erotic and sensual. He explained to her that he really wasn't a dancer he was an actor and needed to work at Mahoganys until he got his big acting break. The lovely lady smiled and told him that she could help him get an acting job, because she worked for a television producer, who had a successful TV series on the air. She was this producer's executive assistant and she got the job through the producer's wife with whom she was very close friends and roommates in college.

Marian told him she didn't like the producer very much. He was a degenerate and he screwed actresses of all ages and boys and anything else he could stick his penis into, except his wife. Robert told Marian that he wasn't interested in having sex with a man just to get a job. She laughed and told him that he didn't have to. All he had to do was to go to bed with her and service the producer's wife who could get him work on her husband's TV series.

So he bedded the lady Marian and attended to the producer's wife's needs. That got him a job on the TV show, a three line part. He had no problems with the producer, who was very nice to him.

After that Marian's friend wanted to help him, so she had turned Robert on to another lonely producer's wife. That's how it all began. A daisy chain of lonely, neglected producer's wives that he hoped could eventually lead him to   movie stardom.

Robert now focuses back to Diana. "Oh, about that lady I met at Mahoganys, the one who told me what I had to do, to make it in this town. I took her advice. She was my first client, that's how I got to you. A friend in need, another friend in need and so on," confesses Robert, who wasn't ashamed of his beginings.

"I see," says Diana who understood where Robert was coming from. Diana sighed, stared at Robert for a moment and firmly vowed, "I can and I will help you Robert. I know other neglected wives like me who can use your marvelous services and they will also help your career. In fact, Joe Canin the producer is having a big party on Saturday. It's for his just completed movie. Harry and I have been invited. Everybody who's anybody in the movie business will be there, including an Arab Sheik, who's the Oil Minister of one of those Arab countries. I can get you on the guest list," says Diana honestly.

Robert is surprised and impressed. With a big grin on his face, he asks Diana, "How?"

"Canin's wife Ellen," replies Diana. "She is one of us. After I tell her what a great talent you are she will be dying to meet you. I know she is going to like you very, very, much."

Robert smiles and gently pulls Diana down to him. "You're a lovely women and I love to make love to you, even if you don't get me the job."

Robert kisses her with great passion. Diana sighs, coos and responds to his compliment with a great French kiss. She takes hold of his manhood and plays with it. Immediately it becomes rigid. She moves down to his crotch and slowly but gently starts to lap every inch of his balls, then Diana's tongue darts its way up to the head of his shaft. A slow moaning sound of gratification comes out of Robert's throat. Diana takes a deep breath and quickly engulfs her mouth over his large cock taking every inch of it into her throat without even gagging. He is in heaven and so is Diana. Each time Robert's penis slides in and out of Diana's saliva wet mouth, he moans and groans in ecstasy. Robert's euphoria excites Diana. She sighs each time Robert's penis hits the bottom of her throat. Diana just loves sucking a cock. Her fond memories swiftly took her back to when and how she learned the great techniques of giving great head. It was when she worked as a model back East. She was sharing an apartment in New York City with one of the top models in the business, Cindy North. Cindy taught her everything she knew about sex. She let Diana know that if she wasn't careful when having straight sex, she could become pregnant. That condition could ruin her body and thus would end her modeling career. So cock-sucking was at the top of their list and that specialty, plus their beauty got them a hell of a lot of modeling work. Her husband Harry told her that she was the best penis eater he's ever had. That's why she always thought was the reason for Harry marrying her. Men, do love to have their dicks sucked and Diana just adored doing it to them. It gave her power and a tremendous orgasm.

Diana was so happy when Harry moved her into his expensive fifteen room Southern California Belaire estate, a place where the rich and famous resided. He gives her a brand new red Mercedes every year. Diana was a good wife, she loves him very much. She never cheated on him until she caught him in bed with one of the top movie stars in Hollywood, Sharon Rock. Harry gave Diana a justifiable excuse, "Rock wouldn't star in my picture unless I fucked her and paid her $12 Million in salary." "Bullshit," cried Diana and that was the end of that story. The picture made a lot of money and that's what it's all about, money. Since then she and Harry have had an understanding. He can sleep with anyone he wanted to and so could she. It now was a marriage of convenience.

Even though Diana's thoughts were of the past, she could feel Robert's slippery throbbing penis in her mouth get as hard as marble. She knew that he was ready to come and in a heart beat she sent her mind forward to the present. Diana's flawless skill brought Robert to an tremendous, marvelous orgasm. Diana swallowed every drop of his love juice. "Oh, Robert, I loved it. It was just what I needed, it was awesome," declares Diana about her accomplishment.

Robert takes the beautiful Diana into his arms and whispers into her ear, "Diana, you're beautiful and so fantastic. I honestly like you very much."

"I feel the same about you Robert," Diana says cooing like a little girl. "You know Diana, I'm really looking forward to seeing you again and meeting your husband Harry at Canin's big party on Saturday night," says

Robert with anticipation in his voice. Robert presses his lips to the lovely Diana's lips and gives her a long, moist, passionate kiss and the foreplay starts all over again.

Chapter Two
Aunt Bea's House

It is four in the afternoon and the Southern California summer sun is blazing brightly, while its rays hit the wind-shield of a faded silver colored 1992 Toyota Carolla coming down, a North Hollywood street. When the vehicle reaches the end of the street it turns into the driveway of a modest early forties ranch Robert Anthony steps out of the Toyota, he is carrying a large bag of groceries. He prances to the front entrance of the building, unlocks the door and enters the house.

Robert moves through the clean, orderly, small six Room house, which is furnished and decorated with simplicity. Robert gets to a nice sized kitchen that is equipped with all the necessary hardware for cooking and baking. He sets his large bag of groceries down on the tiled counter and digs into the sack. He takes out a gallon of milk, a head of lettuce, a small bag of tomatoes, two "T" bone steaks, a six pack of beer, soda and a large saran-wrapped beef bone. He places all of the items into the refrigerator and then moves to the kitchen window that is over the sink. He pulls aside the window curtain and glances through the spotlessly clean pane of glass that looks out to the back yard. His eyes search around the large, lush green flower blooming garden with its fruit bearing trees. He see his aunt Beatrice Turner, she's a thin pretty lady in her fifties standing on a ladder, picking large beautiful peaches from the tree and placing them into a half filled basket. Then his eyes move to Sam a dark brown setter dog of about six years old, lying in the shaded area of an orange tree, with his eyes closed. Robert smiles warmly and goes out of the kitchen back door that leads into the yard.

WILLIAM HELLINGER

The sound of the kitchen door closing turns his aunt Bea's head in a flash. She shouts, "Bobby," when she sees her nephew.

Sam's eyes flip open, when he hears aunt Bea yell Robert's name. Sam jumps to his feet, tail spinning he runs to Robert, leaps up on him and licks his masters face. Aunt Bea starts down the ladder with her basket of peaches. Robert grabs the basket from his aunt, gives her a warm loving smile and carefully helps her down the ladder. Robert places the basket of peaches on the ground and kisses his aunt on the cheek, "Aunt Bea, you know I don't like you climbing ladders. I told you when I get home I will do all the picking of fruit you needed," says Robert firmly.

Aunt Bea caresses her nephew's face, "I know you did, Bobby, but I finished my housework and laundry early, so I had some time on my hands and," Robert cuts his aunt off, "What if there was a six point quake while you're up there picking those beautiful peaches?"

"Well then, just bury me where I fall," states Aunt Bea soberly. They look at each other and break out into laughter.

"Bobby, I can't worry about earthquakes. Sure the big one's coming, but I've got to get my fruit off my trees before the birds and bugs get to them. If not there would be no fruit left for me to do my canning, make you preserves, bake you pies, cakes and jello cocktails," says Aunt Bea seriously.

Robert shakes his head as a sign of surrender. He is well aware that his Aunt Bea is an independent woman with a mind of her own and a native Californian to boot.

Robert smiles lovingly and puts his arm around his aunt, "Aunt Bea, how about one of your peach pies for dinner?"

"Bobby, I've already prepared two pie crusts for you," declares a grinning Aunt Bea. Robert gives her a big kiss on both of her cheeks and on her forehead for good measure. Aunt Bea's eyes are moist with happiness, she loves he nephew, he is the most important thing in her life. She would do anything for him he is her weakness and has been since she raised him from a baby.

THE FIRST LADY

Bea's mind rolls back to when she was contacted by the North Hollywood Police. She was her sister's only living relative and the police informed her of the tragic accidental deaths of her sister and brother-in-law and how her baby nephew survived. She was devastated, heart broken. The state wanted to place Robert into an orphanage, because Bea was unmarried and was trying to make it as an actress in Hollywood.

Bea was living in the house that her father had left to her and her sister. Before all this tragedy occurred she was working nights as a bartender in Hollywood. She had saved enough money from the job to go to New York to live, and try to get acting jobs in the theater, but that was short lived. Now Bea had a home, a job, some money and let the state know that she would give up her acting career to raise her nephew Robert. She wanted her sister's child and wouldn't take "no" for an answer, but she was declined.

That didn't discourage Bea. She went to all the city and state agencies that had the say-so in an orphan child's life. She pleaded with them and begged them to let her have her sister's child. Again, they turned her down. She was destroyed, she didn't know where, or who to turn to for help. She was depressed and cried herself to sleep every night.

Then one night when she was working at the bar, a friend, an old character actor she had worked with on a picture came into the bar. He told Bea his troubles and she told him her troubles. It seemed that his problems could be shelved at the moment. Robert was the old actor's primary concern and told Bea to go see a dear friend of his who was a City Councilman.

That's what Bea did. The Councilman advised her to go up to Sacramento and see a certain State Senator an old friend of his who owed him a big favor. So Bea went up to the State Capital and after a dozen times trying to contact the Senator she finally got to see him. He saw that Bea was young, attractive and desperate. The peoples choice, 'the bastard'. He told her he could help her if she would go away with him.

Bea agreed to spend a weekend with him at his hideaway in Carmel. A weekend of sex didn't shock Bea. She was twenty-nine and particular who she went to bed with. But this was different. She would fuck the Devil if she could get her nephew and keep him. Bea did the trick and she got Robert. Until this day, no one knows what Beatrice Turner had

WILLIAM HELLINGER

to do to get her nephew, especially Robert. Since then, Bea has been very religious. Bea's recall faded when Robert hugged her. "Aunt Bea," says Robert in a child like voice, "I can't eat two pies tonight."

"Don't worry Bobby, you'll eat the other pie for breakfast," says Aunt Bea knowingly. They both laugh.

Then Aunt Bea asks him, "How did your interview go with that casting lady today?"

"Oh, it just went great," he quickly replies. "She liked me, I'm almost sure I got the part," says Robert with confidence.

"That's just wonderful Bobby." she says excitedly.

"The film is going to be shot in Montana and you're going to come on location with me."

"I'd like that," says Aunt Bea happily.

"Aunt Bea, I've got a feeling that this is going to be my big break," Robert says with great assurance.

Aunt Bea is so elated she does a jig and declares, "I'm so happy for you and I'm sure good things are in your future."

"Oh and there is something else I've got to tell you," says Robert.

Aunt Bea is wide eyed with Robert's anticipation of more good news.

"The casting lady knows Joe Canin the big Producer and she got me invited to his big Hollywood party on Saturday night," says Robert who feels very guilty about lying to his Aunt Bea. He couldn't really tell her how he accomplished his good fortune.

"That's really great news, You'll meet a lot of important people there who could help you with your career," says his aunt who is extremely ecstatic. "I wish your mom and dad were here to see all this. But I know they're looking down from Heaven," continues Aunt Bea with a religious tone in her voice.

"I hope not," and with speed Robert catches himself. "I mean I know they are Aunt Bea," Robert says with reverence.

Aunt Bea's lips tighten, "They were too young to die, damn that hit and run driver!"

Robert tries to keep his aunt from being upset, "Don't dwell on it Aunt Bea, that was a long time ago."

Bea almost breaks out into tears, "Yes, but it's so hard to forget, I loved them very much."

Robert hugs his aunt tightly and tells her, "I wish I could have known them. But, I've got you Aunt Bea and I'm always going to take care of you. Now, I want you to go in and take a nap. I'll change my clothes and pick the rest of the peaches you need." He puts his arm around his aunt's waist, "Hey Aunt Bea, I got us a couple of "T" bones for dinner." Robert pats his dog on the head and says to the K—9, "Sam, I've got a present for you too."

Sam 'barks' a happy thanks while his tail gyrates in anticipation. Aunt Bea smiling broadly says, "You're such a good boy, Bobby.

I'm so proud of you." She kisses him on the cheek.

They head for the house with Sam leading the way. When the happy trio reach the kitchen door, Aunt Bea makes a request.

"Oh Bobby, could you bring back a copy of FOREST GUMP from the store tonight, I want to see it again, is that alright?"

"Ah, well, yes, of course Aunt Bea. I'll bring you that and three brand new hits that we just got in," says Robert laughing to cover up another one of his lies.

"Oh, Bobby, you're such a good boy. I do love you."

Chapter Three
Saturday Night Arrives

The bright glow from the full moon reveals a fifteen room rambling mansion on a hillside. It sits on four immaculately groomed green acres. A high Spanish designed wrought iron picket wall surrounds the lush property. The entrance to the grounds, have large iron doors that operate electronically. They are the only entry and exit to the large estate.

This Utopian enclave is the home of Hollywood's most successful movie producer, Joe Canin. Before the last Los Angeles major earthquake this vast lush estate was valued at 22 Million. In today's real estate market it has tumbled down to 18 Million and Canin, who's very rich, doesn't give a good crap.

It all started for Canin when he made a low budget movie after he graduated from U.C.L.A. in the '70s with a BA in film production. That picture was a Box office success world wide. This phenomena of course, impressed the major film studios. All the major VIPs tried to make production deals with this young genius, but Joe Canin did deals on his own terms. In 25 years of movie making Canin never made an unsuccessful film and for Tinsel Town that was an astounding record.

As for his marriage record, Canin was unsuccessful, just plain lousy. He screwed young starlets by the dozens, while he worked his ass off putting pictures into production. Canin's busy activities made his wife Ellen just another neglected Hollywood trophy and that's about all that can be said about Joe Canin. Except, he throws the greatest Hollywood parties and tonight's big bash is no exception. All the lights are ablaze around the property. Music, laughter and the din of Joe's guests are rollicking that emotes through out the manor.

    Guests are still arriving at Canin's Saturday night party. Two chauffeur driven cars are coming though the entrance of the huge wrought iron gates of the massive estate. The vehicles roll up the circular driveway and pass a water fountain which has a variety of colored lights built into it. They give the fountain's gushing waters that magic rainbow illusion.

    When the vehicles pull up to the entrance of the large mansion, there are two waiting uniformed car valets who move to the limo and drive them to the large parking area at the other side of the manor.

    The formally dressed passengers walk up the Italian marble steps to the vast teakwood doors of the mansions entrance. There stands a well-built young man, a Swartzinagger double, positioned at the open doors to greet the guests. They give the security man their invitations. Who then finds their names on the guest list, checks them off and lets them enter the house.

    Robert's faded silver Toyota is close behind a late model white Rolls Royce that is moving through the entrance gates of the Canin estate. His old Japanese car tails the expensive white limo to the entrance of the house. The valet boys see both cars and they sprint to the white Rolls first. The looser valet moves to Robert's old car, gives him a look of disdain. But Robert keeps his cool, offering the valet a big smile and tells the man, "Don't worry, it won't bite you. It only eats sushi," as he laughs. The valet doesn't respond to Robert's humor. Smoothly, Robert digs into his pocket and gives the man a five dollar tip. The valet looks at the money and gives Robert a broad smile, "Oh thank you sir, I'll see your car gets a good parking spot." He gets into the Toyota and carefully drives Robert's car to the parking area.

    Two large bodyguards, Karim and Abdullah, about thirty years of age are standing at attention at the rear door of the white Rolls Royce. They are dressed in fine Arab garb. Sheik Ali Seid the Arab Oil Minister of Bokuf, steps out of the limo. He is about fifty, slight, thin, homely man, with an enormous nose. The Sheik lives in a Palace a few miles from Harut City, Bokuf's capital. His family had been in residence at the Palace since it was built by his clan's ancestry centuries ago. Not far from his Palace, Seid has a five-thousand acre date farm and horse ranch. In the center of this fertile desert property is a small lake, which is fed by an underground water shed.

Sheik Seid's country was never colonized by any foreign power, because it was the poorest and the smallest nation of all the Arab lands. And its pastoral people preferred to graze goats and sheep rather than to work the land, only few farmed their land. King Jamal's royal clan had ruled the country of Bokuf with iron fists for over a hundred years and they taxed the people heavily so they could live in royal splendor maintaining their large Harem's. Then five years ago the largest oil deposits in all of the Arab Republics were discovered in Bokuf. That's when Sheik Seid was made the oil minister and the nation joined OPEC and things quickly changed in Bokuf. All the people were put on fixed incomes and they shared the oil wealth. Now they are very content, not wanting for anything and so they love their ruler and would never think of overthrowing the monarchy. King Jamal and his adviser's knew that a monthly dole to its citizens would keep them docile, serene and agreeable with their government's policies.

As Sheik Seid, moves aside, Jasmine a beautiful Arab girl of eighteen with a magnificent figure, steps out of the Rolls. The Sheik takes her arm and guides her up the steps with his bodyguards closely behind them.

Robert moves up the steps following the Sheik's party. Jasmine turns her head, catching a glimpse of Robert and smiles at him. He returns a friendly smile to this beautiful young Arab girl.

The Sheik is not aware of this exchange between Jasmine and Robert for his attention is diverted by the big security man with the guest list, who is giving the Sheik an over zealous welcome of importance. Seid smiles broadly and acknowledges the young man's royal greeting. The Sheik, and his entourage step into the mansion.

Robert is aware of the fuss the big security man had given to the Sheik and he gives the keeper of the list a big confident smile. The big man blocks his way and speaks arrogantly to him, "Your name?"

"Robert Anthony!" Robert replies with aplomb. Robert holds his breath as the suspicious man scans the list. When he finds Robert's name his face registers disappointment. He checks Robert's name off the list and mumbles dryly, "Anthony, yeah! Yours is the last name on the list."

WILLIAM HELLINGER

Robert, with self-assurance and broad smile tells the guardian of the invited names, "I know I should have been listed with the 'A's but, it was a last minute invitation." Robert turns away, giving the man with egg on his face a titter.

The disillusioned monitor of the list reluctantly moves away from the entrance, as Robert goes past the big man and moves into the lavish carpeted foyer inside the house. Immediately, he sees Joe Canin. He's a bald, heavy set man of medium height standing underneath the ornate crystal chandelier that hangs from a domed ceiling in the large foyer.

Ellen Canin is a tall, lovely blonde of thirty two, with a great body. She stands next to her husband, who is engaged in a conversation with Sheik Seid. Ellen was one of Joe's starlets he had under a three year contract. She was a pretty good actress, but when she married Joe, she gave it all up to be his good wife. The first two years of their marriage was great for her, but then things changed for Ellen, neglect set in. Joe got tired of screwing Ellen and he went back to his old habits banging starlets who wanted an acting job from him. To date he had worn out three casting couches.

Jasmine stands at Sheik's Seid's side smiling warmly, while his bodyguards flank them. Robert gives Jasmine a friendly smile as he moves past the group and goes into the party room.

"By the way Sheik Seid, did you get to read my screenplay?" inquires Canin.

"Yes, mister Canin," he replies with an Arab English accent. "Yes I have, I like it very much. I will see that you have all of the co-operation you need when you come to Bokuf to film your marvelous story. In fact I might be interested in investing in your production."

Canin playing it cool replies, "Thank you Sheik Seid, it's very good of you to help me with my film, but as for your investing I already have the financing from a major studio. However, if you really want to, I can sell you a few of my points."

The Sheik is perked up and says, "Well yes, we can discuss that and also a possibility of buying out your major investor."

Canin had played this business game many times. "That might be possible. It would give me more control of my film," he pauses then he continues, "Alright.", insists the Sheik.

"Ali, let's go up to my study where we'll discuss it, if that's alright with you."

"Yes, that would be good for me," says the Sheik with a serious expression on his face. He turns to his bodyguards and in Arabic says, "Abdullah, you will come with me. Karim, you stay with Jasmine." The bodyguards nod in compliance to their Sheik, while Jasmine smiles. Then Seid turns to Canin, "Okay Joe, let's go talk."

Ellen tries to be a good host, so with a friendly smile she volunteers a suggestion to the Sheik, "Sheik Seid, while you're busy I'll show your daughter around, introduce her to all my friends, if that's alright with you."

The Sheik smiles confidently and declares, "Yes, Mrs. Canin that would be very nice of you, but Jasmine is not my daughter, she will soon be my wife."

Ellen tries to cover her mistake with a big smile. Canin and the Sheik who are still smiling, walk to a winding stairway that leads up to his study and other rooms. They proceed up the steps with Abdullah following them.

Ellen doesn't know what to say to Jasmine, so she just smiles. Jasmine, smiling back says, "Mrs. Canin, I would enjoy meeting your friends." Ellen takes Jasmine's arm and the two lovely women move into the party room, with Karim not too far behind them. Other guests came in and out the foyer into the happy, noisy, crowded room.

The gala room is enormous it is filled with men and women of every age. Some are dressed informally, while others are in formal attire. There are patches of guests around the room who are engaged in conversation. Other visitors are just milling about or serving themselves at the two festively decorated tables where food, fruit, and desserts of every kind are spread out. Some people are lined up at the long bar, drinking, or being served by the three bartenders who attend the well stocked bar.

WILLIAM HELLINGER

Servants and maids move through the room, with each of them carrying a tray of hors d'oeuvres and wine and they offer them to the happy guests. The nice soft music that is being played in the room comes from five musicians who are on a small bandstand. Couples are dancing to the music on a make-shift dance floor in front of the stage.

Robert is balancing a drink in his hand as he makes his way through the crowded room, trying to avoid spilling his drink. A thought comes to mind, "What if I spill my drink on some Icon or anyone else. It could get me thrown out of this who's who get together and I may never get another chance to try and pierce the almost impossible, impenetrable 'Celluloid Jungle'." With a wing and a prayer he finally gets to a lesser congested area near the rooms enormous fireplace then breathes a deep sigh of relief.

Robert edges a little closer to the big hearth. Then he scans the room to see if he can spot Diana among the guests, but he has no luck. Robert is thirsty and when he lifts his glass to drink his ginger ale one of the waitresses, a long legged twenty-one year old beauty, with a sensational body to match, smiles at him and offers him goodies from her tray.

"Sir, would you care for an hors d'oeuvre?" says the girl very sweetly. Robert smiles and shakes his head 'no'. The girl leans slightly forward revealing her good sized breasts to Robert, and says in a whispered breath, in a Monroe like tone voice.

"I'm sure they're really very tasty. I helped make them,"

Robert couldn't help getting a good panoramic view of the lovely girl's nice hooters and he gives them a grand smile of approval. He reached for a canapé. "Home made, huh? I'll try one," says Robert who takes a bite of the hors d'oeuvre and says, "Mmm, they are really good."

The young waitress smiles and says, "Thanks." Then she confidentially reveals to Robert, "You know, I don't really do this kind of work. I'm really an actress and a darn a good one."

Robert smiles, then a thought strikes him, "Mmm, maybe this girl thinks I'm a producer or a casting agent."

THE FIRST LADY

The girl leans closer to Robert and whispers to him, "You see, my agent knows this caterer and that's how I got this job. She told me I could meet a lot of important movie people here who could help my career. So if you're a producer or casting agent, I can read for you anywhere you want me to at any time," she then gives him a hinting smile.

Robert hesitates for a moment, then says in a sotto voce, "I'm sorry, ah, Miss,"

"My name is Lorna Britain."

"Robert Anthony is mine Lorna. I wish I could help you, but I'm an actor myself looking for my big break."

The aspiring young girl is a little disappointed, but with a smile says, "Robert, you're very honest and very nice. If you ever want to get together, I'll give you my phone number, okay?"

Robert likes the girls honesty, her beauty and her great young body. "Yes, I'd like that very much," he says with expectation.

Lorna gives Robert her phone number and says, "I hope you'll remember the number and call."

"Lorna, I'll never forget you," says Robert with a sincere smile as he reaches for another one of her canapés, "Or your number, 555-3669."

"Robert, you're awesome and I can't wait for us to get together," declares the happy brunette. Robert gives her a big smile and nods his head affirmatively. The young girl gives Robert a big good luck smile and goes off.

Robert observes the luscious Lorna as she moves through the crowd portraying her role as a waitress. He smiles sympathetic-
ally, takes a bite of the canapé and downs the rest of his ginger ale. He sets the empty glass and his unfinished hors d'oeuvre on the shelf of the fireplace.

Robert moves into the crowd searching the room and hoping to find Diana. His eyes fall on Ellen Canin and the beautiful, young Arab girl with her bodyguard who is standing by her protectively.

WILLIAM HELLINGER

Ellen is introducing the girl to some of her guests. Robert smiles to himself and is about to move off when he sees Diana Stuart come into the room through the open doors of the patio. With her is a tall, nice looking man in his forties, who is obviously her husband Harry. He trails close behind her. The two move through the crowd waving their greetings to the people they know.

Robert meanders through the crowded room trying to reach them. With a happy smile she waves back to him. She and Harry walk to where Robert is and when they get to him, Diana gives Robert a luscious smile and a big hug.

When Harry sees the way his wife greets this young stud he forces a knowing smile to Robert.

"Robert, how are you?" purrs Diana slowly.

"Real fine." exclaims Robert brightly.

"I'm so happy you could make it." Diana chimes. "I wouldn't have missed this marvelous party for anything Diana. Thanks for getting my name on the list," says Robert with an appreciative smile.

"Are you enjoying yourself?" Diana counters warmly.

"Yes, very much and there are so many important people in the business here." replies Robert excitedly.

"Yes, I know," says Diana laughing.

"It would take me a hundred years to try and get to them for a job and that's a fact," states Robert.

"Well, now you won't have to wait that long Robert, this is Harry my husband," declares Diana.

"I was looking forward to meeting you, Mister Stuart." says Robert, with an acceptable professional honesty. "I've heard so much about you, Mister Stuart," continues Robert as he holds out his hand.

THE FIRST LADY

Harry extends his and with a half-way smile shakes Robert's hand. "And I heard about you Robert," says Harry who knows the score. Diana grinning nods her head to Robert.

"Diana tells me among other things, that you're a very fine actor," declares Harry who had been programmed by Diana. Robert smiles proudly and stands attentively.

"I'm doing a film in Montana, there are a couple of roles you could play, damn good parts," Harry says this knowing that he has to. He takes his business card out of his handkerchief pocket, hands it to Robert and gives his wife a quick look with a smile. Diana shoots a 'that's a good boy' smile back to her husband.

"Come see me on Monday, I'll give you a script to read," says Harry in summation.

"Thanks, Mister Stuart," replies Robert very pleased as he gives Diana a very big, 'you really did it' grateful smile. "What time do you want me to be at your office, Mister Stuart?" Stuart replies, "Three o'clock will be fine, oh, you will have to cut your hair for the part," Harry, really enjoys telling that to the big stud. "Okay with you, Robert?" he says smiling.

"Sure, sure, of course!" confirms Robert without any hesitation. Again Robert smiles thankfully to his benefactor. Diana returns a triumphant smile to Robert. Just then, Ellen and Jasmine, followed by her bodyguard Karim, approached the trio.

"Di! Harry!" bubbles Ellen with great enthusiasm, "I'm so happy that you both could make it!"

"Oh Ellen, we wouldn't have missed this party for anything," says Diana with gusto.

"I'll second that Ellen!" agreed Harry. "Where's Joe?" inquires Harry.

"In a meeting with Sheik Seid, about money matters. He won't be too long Harry," confides Ellen.

Jasmine keeps eyeing Robert from the moment she arrived with Ellen. He becomes uneasy by this beautiful Arab girl staring at him.

"Diana, Harry, this is Jasmine the Sheik's." Jasmine quickly cuts Ellen off and with a sweet, cool, slight Arab accent, "His daughter. Yes, I am Sheik Seid's daughter."

Ellen was a little puzzled by Jasmine's self introduction. She thinks to herself. Why did Jasmine say she was the Sheik's, daughter. Then she notices Jasmine's eyes fixed on the good looking young man. She concludes that Jasmine wants to play with him, while the Sheik is busy. She is enjoying this. Ellen doesn't give a 'gnats' ass to what Jasmine does, it's none of her business anyway. Besides, who is she to throw the first brick. Ellen relishes her power for a moment. She sees that Jasmine's eyes are glued to her and is holding her breath in anticipation of what her answer will be. So Ellen decides to play along with Jasmine's temporary blood tie to Sheik Seid.

With a sincere smile Ellen confirms Jasmine's little white lie. "Yes, yes, of course, his younger daughter."

Jasmine gives Ellen a grateful look and a thank you smile. "This is Karim my bodyguard," says Jasmine graciously. The big, perfectly built man stands behind his charge with his large muscular arms folded. A dead-panned expression is fixed on his dark, sun-tanned colored face. Robert, Diana and Harry are extremely impressed with Jasmine's protector. They all acknowledge Karim, with respectful smiles.

"Oh Ellen, Jasmine," Diana states pointedly, "This is Robert Anthony." Jasmine smiles warmly and nods her head to Robert with interest. No one notices Harry turn his head away when he sees the three women fawning over the young stud, he yawns with boredom.

Ellen is surprised, "So this is Robert, the young man Diana had told me about. Oh Robert, hello," says Ellen with a big knowing smile of joy.

"Mrs. Canin, Jasmine, nice meeting you both," Robert says smiling in a gentlemanly fashion.

THE FIRST LADY

Ellen queries Robert with a more sensual tone in her voice, "Diana tells me, that you're a fine actor and a marvelous dancer too."

Robert is a little embarrassed and gives Ellen a broad smile.

Diana smiling winks to Ellen. "He's very modest Ellen, I can vouch for Robert's big talent." Ellen and Diana laugh knowingly. Jasmine, smiles. Harry, with a 'fuck you all' smile announces, "Well ladies it's been nice, but I have to leave you. I see someone I must talk to." Harry gives Diana a forced smile, then turns to Robert, "Don't forget Monday at three, Robert." Harry really hated to tell him that but this is showbiz. Harry quickly moves off, disappearing into the crowd.

Robert now feels awkward standing with the three women. Ellen is aware of his uneasiness and smiles, "We have to go too. Robert, it was nice meeting you. I do hope to see you again, very, very soon," says Ellen sweetly in anticipation. Robert smiles and parallels with Ellen's thoughts, "I'm sure we'll run into each other, real soon I hope and thank you for having me here."

"You're welcome Robert, I'm sure one day you'll show me "Ellen, you can count on him," says Diana. Then, almost in a whisper Diana sensually volunteers her opinion, "And Ellen, he is such a great lover," she whispers. Robert's face becomes slightly crimson and he turns his head away.

Diana and Ellen notice Robert's reaction and giggle, but Jasmine just gives a lady like smiles.

Ellen takes Jasmine's hand and starts to leave.

"Mrs. Canin!" says Jasmine quickly, "Would you mind if I do not go with you?"

"But," Ellen knowingly has to say this, so with phony concern "I told the Sheik that I would look after you until he and my husband finished their business."

"Thank you, Mrs. Canin, but I will be alright. Karim is here," says Jasmine with an assuring smile.

Ellen's eyes refer to Robert and she smiles knowingly and acting beautifully says, "Okay, if you insist."

"But I do and I thank you again for your kindness and your concern," says Jasmine with social gratitude.

Diana also knows Jasmine's objective and asks Ellen, "Do you mind if I tag along with you?"

"Of course not Di, I'd love it."

Diana turns to Robert with an advising, encouraging tone in her voice, "And Robert, don't you forget to do some networking."

"Thanks to both of you, especially you Diana," Robert says gratefully.

The two female advocates smile at Robert's candor. When they move off Ellen and Diana are heard saying, "Di, wait till I show you what I bought at Gucci's today." "I just can't wait." replies Diana excitedly, "and I hope it was very expensive."

"Extremely expensive!" says Ellen with glee. They both roll out joyful laughs and they were suddenly lost in the assembly of guests.

Robert's eyes roll back from the women's departure and interchange. Jasmine is not shocked by the remarks made by the American ladies.

Robert looks at Jasmine and smiles, not knowing what to say except, "Well, it was nice meeting you, I." Robert stares at Jasmine intently, "You're very lovely," confesses Robert. He turns to leave with eyes still fixed on Jasmine. "Please don't go, Robert," pleads Jasmine. This stops Robert cold in his tracks and he turns to her.

Softly Jasmine murmurs, "You are very handsome and I want you to stay and join me in having a drink and some refreshments, that is if you want to."

Robert is very flattered by Jasmine's comment and request. "Yes, I would really like that," lowering his voice. "But, what about your bodyguard?" questions Robert respectfully.

"Do not be concerned about Karim," says Jasmine with assurance, "I can manage him." Jasmine turns to Karim, smiles and in Arabic and gives an order to the big man. "Karim, get us some food." Then she points to the open doors of the patio. "We will be out on the patio."

Karim does not move. "Sheik Seid might not like you being with this infidel," he states in Arabic.

Jasmine begs prettingly, "Please Karim my friend. I just want to enjoy myself before we go home. Please do not say anything to the Sheik."

Karim softens, "Well, alright Jasmine. But please be very careful," warns the big man in a warm friendly tone of voice. Jasmine smiles thankfully and nods her head to Karim.

Karim returns a protective smile and goes to get the refresh- ments. There is a long line of guests waiting to eat.

"Jasmine, what was that all about?" asks Robert who was a little puzzled what Jasmine had said to her bodyguard in her native language.

"I told Karim to get us some food and bring it to us on the patio."

"That sounds good to me," Robert joyfully replies. Robert takes Jasmine's arm and guides her through the throngs of guests, playfully acting the interference game for her. Unscathed they pull up to the open doors of the patio.

"Jasmine you wait here and I'll get us something to drink."

The young girl, smiling softly asks, "Robert, could you get us some champagne?"

"Good choice. I'll get a bottle of their best," answers an eager Robert.

WILLIAM HELLINGER

"I love champagne, it makes me feel so happy and it makes me feel so sexy." Robert stops abruptly, coughing slightly.

"Are you alright?" says Jasmine concerned.

"Yes, the cigarette smoke in here, I'm just a little allergic," says Anthony as he clears his throat. "Jasmine don't move or talk to anyone," Robert acts protective. I'll be right back, okay?" The young girl nods her head and gives Robert an assuring smile.

Robert gets to the bar where people are waiting to be served. One of the bartenders is opening up a bottle of expensive champagne and setting it into a bucket. When Robert sees the bucket of iced champagne sitting on the bar he quickly digs into his pocket and extracts a twenty-dollar bill. Before the bartender can offer the bucket of wine to the waiting guest, Robert, jams the twenty-dollar bill into his hand, takes the iced champagne and two clean glasses on the bar. "Thanks bartender," says Robert respectfully.

The bartender is about to protest, but the money in his palm stops him. "Thank you sir," says the bartender smiling as he stuffs the money into his pocket.

Robert starts for Jasmine and moves carefully with the cold liquid ambrosia.

Jasmine is very surprised to see Robert back so quickly and with her favorite wine too. She smiles happily, grabs his arm tightly and moves through the open doors of the patio.

Chapter Four
Revelation & Seduction

Robert and Jasmine both exclaim that they are in awe when they see the different moving colored lights. Banners and expensive decorations hang over the large patio that overlooks an Olympic size pool. The pool was void of bathers, but there were guests seated at tables that had been placed around the entire area. They are eating, drinking and having a good time.

Robert looks around for an unoccupied table. They see one near the far end of the pool and they head for it. When he and Jasmine get to the table, Robert sets the ice bucket and the champagne down on it and they sit in chairs facing each other.

The nice soft music coming from the house can be heard floating onto the patio. Robert pours the champagne into the two glasses and gives one to Jasmine. They look at each other, smile and make a silent toast as they drink their wine.

"This champagne is excellent, thank you," Jasmine cooed.

"You're welcome, are you enjoying yourself?" Robert replies.

"Oh, yes," says Jasmine giving Robert a big happy smile as she sips her glass of wine she observes in the scenery around her. "I think this place is very pretty. Yes, it is beautiful out here, cool," a deeply sighing Jasmine states as she relaxes with contentment.

"Yes it is, do you get weather like this where you come from?" Robert inquires.

"No, it is hot and dusty in the day and the nights are little cold," replies Jasmine.

"Huh! Where do you come from?"

"Bokuf!" declares Jasmine with a hint of disgust.

"Bokuf? Where is that?" asks Robert curiously.

"It is part of the United Arab Republic, a very, very small country very, very rich in large oil deposits," responds Jasmine like a travel agent.

"Sounds like a very, very interesting country. I just hope while your father is here that he doesn't fall for any Hollywood money schemes," says Robert with some concern.

Jasmine laughs ironically. "Robert, do not be concerned about that. Arabs move very cautiously before they put their money into anything. They investigate the proposition most thoroughly."

Robert stares at Jasmine for a moment. "I see," says Robert with egg on his face. Then he laughs about his misjudgment of how an Arab conducts business. He raises his glass in another toast. "To your beauty, and a safe return home." Robert drinks to Jasmine.

"Thank you, Robert, now for my toast," says Jasmine raising her glass and staring intently at Robert. "Robert, who I wish would make mad love to me," whispers Jasmine with a sincere unabashed sensuality.

Robert is startled by Jasmine's request and he doesn't quite know how to handle this beautiful, young Arab girl's plea. He just gives her a broad smile.

Jasmine cocks her head, licks her lips and get up from her chair. She walks slowly around to the back of Robert's chair. Robert still smiling is silent and he wonders what Jasmine is up to. She stays there for a moment, then places her hand on his head and runs her fingers down his red hair to its tied pony tail.

"Your hair is beautiful, like silk red thread," whispers Jasmine breathlessly.

Robert feels a little awkward and he thinks. Here he is, a guy who's had his share of bedding down women and in all of his encounters, except for the house calls he had made to the ignored wife's of producer's, he has always been the aggressor. This is the first time he has ever been seduced and he thinks that this beautiful young Arab girl's technique is delightfully very smooth. But he better not consider her request, even though he would love to give her a few thrusts, because she is a Sheik's daughter and if Ellen Canin finds out that he spiked Jasmine at her party she is going be angry with him and the shit will 'hit the fan'.

Jasmine seems rejected as she exclaims flatly, "Robert, I did not think that my request would shock you."

Jasmine's blunt and bold request had caught Robert off guard. He laughs, "Well, ah, I don't know what to say Jasmine, why no of course not!" replies Robert playing it cool.

Jasmine slides back to her seat. She stares at Robert for a moment, her eyes twinkle and she gives him a 'Mona Lisa smile'. "Do you not want to make love to me, Robert?" she whispers seductively.

Robert, a little uneasy, shifts in his chair a little and gives Jasmine a smile. "Well, I, oh sure, of course but, I think," Robert hesitates for a moment. He wipes the smile off his face and as he is about to tell her the real reason why it's not a good idea for them to have a 'quicky', Jasmine jumps in with heated fervor continuing her pursuit.

"When I first saw you tonight, my libido tweaked. Then when I met you, I wanted you, very, very much," she boldly admits.

Robert's tension softens, smiling he reaches across the table and takes Jasmine's hand tenderly. "And when I first saw you, I had the same feeling about you, but, you're here with your father, it's too complicated," explains Robert with honesty.

Jasmine feels good with Robert's admission as how he feels about her and she smiles. She grabs the bottle of champagne from the ice bucket. Robert takes it from her and refills her glass and then his.

The young Arab girl slowly raises her glass to her full blown moist lips and downs the entire glass of wine in one gulp. Robert is surprised at Jasmine's action. He follows suit and drains his glass of alcoholic beverage, toute de suite.

Jasmine is now feeling the effects of the champagne her brows furrow. "Robert, what about Diana?" questions Jasmine. Robert again fills his glass with wine and sips it. Jasmine sees that he is avoiding her question regarding Diana and she stares at him. "I heard Diana tell Mrs. Canin that you were a great lover," Jasmine admits.

"Well I...," is all that Robert could get out of his mouth.

Jasmine interrupts him, she is desperate time is running out for her. "I know you must have filled her needs and she must be repaying you by helping you get acting work. There is nothing wrong with that Robert, you give, she gives, that's the barter system," says the Arab girl in a very serious tone of voice. Then Jasmine takes a deep breath and sighs. "When the party is over tonight, I will never see you again. So you must make love to me, I promise I will give you an Arabian night. A night that you will always remember," pleads Jasmine lustfully.

Robert is overwhelmed by this outspoken girl. "You are really something. Do you tell this to every man you want?" He is very inquisitive of this brazen young woman's tenacity.

"Does this bother you, Robert?" declares Jasmine. "Well no, not really, I," utters Robert taking a big gulp of his wine. He stares at this young beautiful Arab goddess for a fleeting moment, "Jasmine, how old are you?" he asks with a try at sobriety.

"Eighteen," answers Jasmine without hesitation.

"You're very mature for your age, smart too. Your father must have sent you to the best schools," Robert says probing.

THE FIRST LADY

"I was educated at the Palace, privately, by the finest educators that money could buy," states Jasmine proudly. Robert isn't too surprised by what this Royal rich girl has just told him. "Your father must be very proud of you," states Robert.

Jasmine's eyes narrow. "It was not my father that got me my education." There is a bitter tone in her voice.

Robert is now extremely puzzled by this girl's declaration. He picks up his glass and downs the rest of his wine.

Jasmine finishes her wine and silently gazes at this man she wants to give herself to. "Sheik Seid, is not my father," confesses Jasmine. "My Father, was poor and when I was thirteen years old he sold me to the Sheik to be one of his wives," recounts Jasmine with moist eyes.

"Oh, you poor kid," Robert says in a stunned manner.

"But now, since the rich oil discovery in my country five years ago, there are no more poor people because the government gives everyone money, whether they work or not. So now, there is no need to sell a girl child to a Sheik for money," says Jasmine ironically.

"Thank God for that." declares Robert.

"But now, there are some who give away their young girls to their Sheik's as a gift for their Harem's."

"Huh! You Arab girls can't win, money or no money."

"Yes and it is very common in some of the other oil rich Arab countries," says Jasmine trying to educate Robert and bring him up to speed on Arab customs and culture.

Robert frowns, shakes his head and pours himself another glass.

Jasmine continues, "But this I must say about Sheik Seid, before he marries a woman for his Harem he gives them all an education first, choosing what they should master in, english, economics, agriculture and other subjects that will help run his business affairs. He has business in his Sheikdom and all around the world. I know he is the only sheik in Bokuf,

WILLIAM HELLINGER

who educates his wives," explains Jasmine with her historic revelation. "That's really something. I must say, that the Sheik is a very clever man. But what if some of the women don't graduate?" asks Robert.

"Then he sends them back to their families," answers Jasmine.

"What did you master in?" inquires Robert.

Jasmine smiles broadly and she responds proudly, "Sexology, I have a degree in sex therapy."

Robert shakes his head and laughs. "I must say, you're full of surprises." Jasmine smiles sweetly. "You must make the Sheik very happy," says Robert with a sexy grin.

The young girl quickly responds indignantly. "I am still a virgin. The Sheik was to marry me in Bokuff, but because he is the oil Minister he had to leave the country to take care of urgent business here in America. In three days we will be married in Washington, your capital. My countries diplomat will perform the ceremony. The Sheik cannot wait to have his virgin lamb."

"I can't blame him," says Robert.

Jasmine's eyes suddenly become wet. She cries out with tears in her eyes and in a low bitter tone in her voice, "He is ugly. I hate him. I always have from the day he took me from my family. Robert, I am so unhappy. I wish I could run far away from him." A gush of tears roll down Jasmine's beautiful face, as she cries softly.

Robert quickly moves to her and places his arms around her to comfort her. "Jasmine, please take it easy. Running away isn't the solution. With all the money and power, that royal bastard has, he'll find you. It might be worse for you, now is not the time," Robert warns the distressed girl. "My advice to you is wait, stick it out, make plans!" Robert's encouraging words quickly brings Jasmine's tears to a halt.

"Oh Robert," Jasmine whispers. "You are, so understanding." She looks into his sympathetic eyes and presses her lips to his lips, very passionately.

Robert responds for a moment then he realizes what Jasmine is up to. He tries to break away from her, but the Arab girl's arms are locked tight around Robert's neck and her lips are fastened to his like a suction cup with her tongue searching his mouth. Robert, enjoying the moment realizes he has to escape her clutches before the Sheik's bodyguard who is supposed to bring them food sees them. He quickly maneuvers himself out of Jasmine's grip, and breaks away breathlessly from her vacuuming lips.

Despite Robert's escape from Jasmine's seductive clutches she turns on him again. This time she leans forward and softly murmurs in his ear. "Robert, I would go away much happier if you would take me now."

Robert backs away from Jasmine, searching for an excuse. "I can't do that you wouldn't be a virgin for him. Then Jasmine, what would you tell the Sheik?"

Jasmine explains very calmly. "The Sheik has a large stable of horses. I go riding almost every morning before breakfast. I will simply tell him, that I lost my virginity with one of his spirited horses," states Jasmine very plain, simple, without fear and with an educated self-assurance.

"He'd believe that?" asks Robert puzzled. "Oh yes, this has happened before with one of his other wife's," answers Jasmine truthfully.

Robert is very surprised. "Will he buy the horse story again?" Robert asks. "Why not, her story was a bicycle," responds Jasmine with a serious look on her face. Robert laughs uproariously and the young Arab girl wonders why.

Robert pours more champagne into both their glasses, then raises his glass of wine in a silent toast and takes a belt. He stares at Jasmine for a moment, then with serious concern asks, "What if the Sheik finishes his business with Canin, before we get back?"

Jasmine is elated as she gives Robert, a happy confident smile, her honest seduction paid off. "Do not worry Robert the Sheik will weigh every aspect of Canin's proposition before he makes up his mind." Then with a big sensual smile, "We will be back with enough time to spare," she says with assurance.

"And what about your bodyguard?" inquires a very concerned Robert.

"Karim will protect me. He will not say a word," Jasmine guarantees Robert.

"You sure have everything covered," responds Robert with a convinced smile. He then thinks for a moment. "Now, the best place is in my car, no one will see us there. I hope you don't mind Jasmine?" Robert asks in an apologetic tone of voice.

"Right now I do not care where you make mad passionate love to me," declares Jasmine the anxious audacious hot pants young virgin girl as she pulls Roberts lips to her hungry lustful moist lips. She kisses him very hard again. Their bodies transfixed. No sounds of heavy breathing comes from either one of them, they resemble Rodin's 'The Kiss'.

The guests at the nearby tables are oblivious to the tabloid embrace of the lovers. They were having a lot of fun eating, drinking and gossiping.

Robert and Jasmine are out of breath. They finally break their clinch and stare at each other as they catch their breaths. Their faces are etched with desire.

Karim comes into the patio carrying two plates full of food. He looks around the patio to see what table his mistress and her companion are sitting at. He spots them at a table, at the far end of the pool. As he heads for them, he sees Robert take Jasmine's hand and leads her to the rear of the patio and disappears around the building.

The big man gets to the table, sets the plates of food on it and goes in the direction where the two were going, following very quiet and with caution.

Robert and Jasmine move into the car filled guest parking area. Karim comes around the back of the house, just in time to see Robert and Jasmine walk in between, and around the fancy cars.

THE FIRST LADY

Robert's eyes search the rows of vehicles for his car and when he sees his silver Toyota parked in the last row of parked cars he and Jasmine head for it.

Karim sees Robert and Jasmine get into a car. The big man waits for a moment then shakes his head from side to side in disappointment. He ponders on what he should do. He doesn't want to let his mistress know that he saw her get into the car with her companion, but he knew what she was going to do and he didn't want to get her in trouble with the Sheik. Karim turns, and moves off toward the patio.

Soft music coming from the party can be heard. In spite of the rolled up windows in the car and the light and shadow patterns are playing on Jasmine who is lying flat on her back in the reclined passenger's bucket seat.

An incandescent full moon was emitting some light and shadows into the interior of the Silver Toyota. Some of the configurations are spilling onto Robert, who is along side of Jasmine. They are kissing each other most passionately. Robert's right arm is wrapped around Jasmine's neck and with his left hand he is feeling up her young sensual shapely body from her thigh's to her lovely breasts. Robert's foreplay is making Jasmine purr like a big female cat in heat.

Jasmine is so turned on by Robert that she grabs for the big bulge in his crouch and strokes it gently. Her caressing hand movements on Robert's joy-stick, is making him sigh with contentment. Their tongues are humping each other's mouths, and they both moan in ecstasy.

Robert slowly pulls up Jasmine's dress to her waist exposing her bare legs and shear bikini's. His lips quickly shift from Jasmine's red-hot juicy lips to her steaming virgin love well. His talented wet tongue travels over Jasmine's young and beautiful shapely thigh's causing her body to squirm with extreme sexual joy.

"Oh, Robert, I knew it would be like this with you," whispers Jasmine, moaning and cooing with pleasure and delight.

Robert hears what Jasmine has said to him. He looks up at the lovely young Arab girl's face and sees that her eyes were closed and she is sensually licking her hot wet lips with her mouth wide open with sounds of joyful sighs coming from her throat.

"Sweet Jasmine, you smell so good. I'm so turned on by you, I could eat you up without a seasoning, or a knife and fork," confesses Robert with a lustful laugh. He wastes no time and goes back to Jasmine, making passionate love with his tongue darting underneath her panties and around her pubic hairs. Robert's wet hot tongue was making Jasmine moan, groan and softly scream. She was about to climax, but Robert was a pro. He knew she was about to come and he withdrew his tongue.

"Oh, Robert!" squealed Jasmine.

Robert pulls off Jasmine's bikini's, raises and spreads her legs, exposing the young girls pink lips.

Karim, Jasmine's loyal guard is tense, worried. He is standing guard at one side of the open patio doors. His eyes are searching every area of the patio hoping for his mistress's quick return, hopefully before the Sheik finds out that his future virgin bride is gone. Karim thinks to himself. What if the Sheik does find out Jasmine is not there with him. He did not want to think of why Jasmine was not there with him. He did not want to think of what his master's wrath could do. But he was sure of one thing. The Sheik would kill the American infidel for offending his royal family and his manhood. Only Allah could know how he would punish Jasmine.

Several party guests agree enjoying the many famous paintings on the walls of the upper floor of the Canin mansion and are commenting on Canin's expensive taste in art. As the art connoisseurs move past Canin's study to the winding stairs to the foyer, Canin's door swings open. Sheik Seid came through the open door to the corridor, followed by Canin and Abdullah the bodyguard.

The trio shift to the stairs and slowly descend them. The Sheik turns to Canin, "Are you sure Joe you can convince Universal to withdraw their financing of your film?" asks the Sheik.

"Ali, I'll just tell them, if they don't do it, I won't make another picture for them. Ali, I know they will agree. I'll sell them some points, that should appease them," chuckles the wily Canin.

THE FIRST LADY

The Sheik plays it cool he laughs to himself and thinks how an Arab has outfoxed the manufacturer of Hollywood films.

When they get down to the foyer Harry Stuart is waiting there.

"Joe, Ellen told me you were tied up in a meeting. Are you free to talk?"

"Sure, Harry," says Canin. "And I want you to meet Sheik Seid, oil minister of Bokuf."

"Sheik Seid," Harry extends his hand to the Arab. "Harry Stuart. It's a real pleasure to meet you," says Harry smiling.

The Sheik takes Harry's hand. "It is also my pleasure, Harry Stuart," recounts the Sheik.

"Ali, Harry is one of my best friends and a damn good movie maker." Seid is impressed. He smiles and nods his head acknowledging Harry's Hollywood status. "Joe, Abdullah and I will go look for Jasmine who is with Mrs. Canin. I will see you later?" declares the Sheik.

"Absolutely, I'll see you before you and leave. I'll have some papers you can take with you to give to your lawyers. Okay?" says Canin with a victorious smile. The Sheik gives an 'okay' gesture with his hand to Canin. Joe and Harry watch the Sheik and his bodyguard go into the party room in search of Jasmine and Ellen.

Karim is still standing guard at the side of open patio doors, with nervous anticipation. His eyes are roaming in all the possible areas that Jasmine could return from. Beads of sweat are beginning to trickle down the big man's face and he wipes his eyes with his big hand. Karim's frustration brings him to a decision, he must go and fetch Jasmine and get her back to the party as quickly as possible.

Just as Karim is about to leave his post, Abdullah comes into the patio and traps him. Abdullah approaches his fellow bodyguard and Karim doesn't know what to tell Abdullah, he just gives the man a forced smile.

"Karim, it is so good to find you so quickly. Mrs. Canin said she saw you get some food for Jasmine and her companion and come out here," says Abdullah while looking around the patio.

"Where is Jasmine?" he asks. "Sheik Seid is waiting for her." Karim is silent, but the look on his face reveals to Abdullah, that something is wrong.

Abdullah's eyes widen and he looks straight into his compatriot's eyes. "Where is she, Karim?" asks Abdullah with a concerned warning tone in his voice.

Unnoticed by his two bodyguards, Sheik Seid enters the patio and overhears what Abdullah has asked Karim. He makes himself conspicuous at the patio doorway. The Sheik notices that Karim is motionless, with a look of nervous apprehension on his face.

But the two men are not aware that their master is listening. Abdullah sees the state that Karim is in and knows something is terribly wrong and his calm look turns into a scowl. "Karim, answer me! Where is Jasmine?" declares Abdullah with great anger.

Karim's face is tight and flushed, his sweating has increased. He tried to answer his friend, but he is tongue tied, then, "I, I, she is, with the American man, they are," blurts Karim. "What are you saying Karim!" says Abdullah in anger. "She is with him in the car," says Karim with fear. "In a car Karim, doing what?" The Sheik now moves forward to his two bodyguards.

His voice frightens the two big men and they turn to see their master is standing behind them.

The Sheik's angry look, makes Karim freeze with fear. He signals Abdullah to pull Karim aside. Abdullah moves Karim into the shadows of the patio just in case there is anything physical applied against Karim. Here the guests who are on the patio will not see or hear what is happening to Karim.

The Sheik orders Abdullah to get Karim down on his knee's. The big bodyguard does his masters bidding.

THE FIRST LADY

The Sheik's eyes are ablaze, he moves his face close into Karim's face. "You were to guard her, stay with her." says the Sheik in a tone that could kill.

"My Sheik, I am sorry. It is my fault I should have not listened to her. She wanted to come out here with the infidel. I am sorry. I was weak. It is my fault, all my fault. Please master, please forgive my stupidity." begs Karim showing fear.

Seid straightens himself up then looks away from Karim. "I will deal with you later," says the Sheik in an ominous, threatening tone of voice. The Sheik turns back to Karim with piercing eyes of anger, "Now take me to where she is."

Robert's silver Toyota is slightly rocking back and forth and from side to side, squeaking with each movement.

Robert is on top of Jasmine, with their lips fastened to each others. Despite Jasmine's virginity, Robert's penetration is total and it made Jasmine cry with pain and joy. She sighs and moans with ecstasy every time he pounded his loins into her vagina. Robert knows that the beautiful Jasmine is ready to have her first and most exciting climax she ever had, by a real live, hard as a rock penis.

The two lovers were about to come at the same time when suddenly the door of the car swings open. Robert and Jasmine are oblivious to the intruders and don't stop their humping rhythm, because they are both having orgasms at the same time.

Jasmine sees Abdullah and Karim each grab one of Robert's arms at the same time. She can't scream, she is stunned and frozen with fright.

Robert tries to protest, but Karim had placed his hand over Robert's mouth. Robert struggles and tries to free his arms but it is no use.

Abdullah swings his massive fist to the back of Robert's neck, giving him a rabbit punch. The powerful blow stops Robert's thrashing, he is out cold, and then there was complete silence in the parking area. The only sounds that can be heard are coming from the house and patio, nice soft music, guests laughing and having fun.

Chapter Five
Robert Has Disappeared

It was Sunday, the following day after the big Hollywood bash that Robert attended. Aunt Bea gets up a little late twelve-noon. She is usually an early riser who gets up at six in the morning like clock-work and with out an alarm going off. But this Saturday night was special for her, because Robert had brought the movie that she had requested. 'FOREST GUMP' and also got her three brand new movie hits. Her nephew spoils her. He was always bringing her movies from Blockmasters. She did not know that Robert wasn't working at Blockmasters any more.

That Saturday night, Aunt Bea had only intended to see two movies, but she saw all four after Robert had left the house for Canin's Hollywood bash. She was in all her glory, she loved films of every kind, any subject matter. She had once been an actress. Aunt Bea always made a ritual out of the night she was to see a movie and this Saturday night was no different than any her other film viewing nights.

Seven P.M. has aunt Bea finishing her cooking of her favorite dinner. She then places the plates of food on a tray and takes it into the living room. Here she sets it down on the coffee table that's facing the television set.

She inserts the first feature into the VCR and sits down on the couch. She punches the play button on the remote. Up comes the credits, titles and the voice of Tom Hanks, is heard coming over the opening scene of the picture. Aunt Bea is very happy. She eats her dinner while watching her very own, 'FOREST GUMP'.

WILLIAM HELLINGER

The fourth feature ends at three AM. with Aunt Bea contented, but bleary eyed. She drags herself to the bedroom, but not before she brushes her teeth, this is the last thing she does before going to bed. Ever since she was a tiny tot, her Grandmother Beatrice, who she was named after, gave her good advice, with a frightening example.

"Honey," said Grandma Bea. "You'll be toothless like me, your Granny." She dug her fingers into her mouth, extracted her upper and lower dentures and displayed them to her grandchild, declaring, "See, that's what happens from eating too many sweets and not brushing after each meal and especially before going to bed. So don't let this happen to you."

Those were sage words and after seeing her Grandmother's false teeth, she brushed her teeth four times a day, sometimes five, always before retiring. She never missed a day. Thanks to Grandma Beatrice, she still has every pearly white tooth in her mouth.

Aunt Bea was asleep before she hit the pillow, she slept soundly until noon. She now felt good and rested as she enjoyed the Saturday night movie fest, "But not again, one picture, or even two will be enough to view for one night," she declares.

Aunt Bea gets on her knees and says her daily prayers very, very quietly. She figured that Robert must have gotten home from the party after she went to bed and she doesn't want to wake him. So she decides to make a Sunday brunch for both of them and when it's ready, she will wake him.

She prepares her nephew's favorites, ham, eggs and waffles. Then she goes to his room, knocks on his closed door and softly calls out. "Robert, it's one o'clock in the afternoon, time to get up and I made your favorite brunch." She waits for her nephew to answer, but there is none. She thinks, maybe Robert doesn't hear because he's real tired from the party. He must be sleeping very soundly. Maybe I should let him sleep. But then if I do that, his brunch will get cold and I will have to throw it away.

Aunt Bea hated to waste good food, so she decides to wake him up. She knew Robert wouldn't be angry with her if she did disturb his sleep to eat his brunch. Besides, she wanted to hear all about Canin's big bash, like who was there, did he meet anyone who could help his acting career, and did he meet any nice young ladies.

Aunt Bea decides to wake Robert. This time she knocks on her nephew's door a little harder and calls out much louder, "Robert!" she says in a sweet lilting tone in her voice. "It's one o'clock and if you want to get up, I've fixed your favorite brunch!" She waits for his response, but there is none. She tries again, but this time, she raps on his door three times, but still there was no reply from Robert. She is puzzled. Then she laughs to herself, she knows that he has heard her and she realizes that Robert might be playing the 'surprise game' on her again.

It was the game she taught him when he was a kid. She would hide in the closet, behind a door, chair or couch and Robert would call her several times and when she didn't answer him he would think she wasn't around. Then when he went past where she was hiding, she would jump out in front of her Robert and yell, "Surprise." and give him a big hug and a kiss. It was a little game of fun that she and his mother had learned when they were little girls.

Robert loved that game and he was great at it, he must be hiding behind the door waiting to yell, "Surprise." grab her and give her a big hug and a sweet kiss. She will play the game, "Yes, let him win", so she opens his bedroom door and she steps into his room smiling and waits for Robert to yell, "Surprise." She waits, but nothing happens. She peers around the door, but Robert isn't there. She looks down to his bed to see if he is making believe he is asleep, but the bed had not been slept in. Now she is a little concerned. But she smiles and figures, Robert must have met a beautiful starlet at the party and spent the night with her. And why not, he is young, handsome, single and an actor with a promising career.

Aunt Bea runs her hand across her nephew's pillow and smiles. She knows that she will see him for supper in the evening, or receive a call from him. So with peace of mind, she eats her Sunday brunch and watches, 'FOREST GUMP' one more time.

Aunt Bea finishes her Sunday chores around the house and those in the yard. When night came she still hadn't heard from Robert. She knows that it isn't like him to be away all this time, without being in touch with her. Now she is a little worried. Maybe she should call the police and tell them that she hasn't heard from her nephew since he left the house

WILLIAM HELLINGER

on Saturday night to attend a party in Beverly Hills. But then she thinks again, maybe the police wouldn't consider Robert a missing person yet. He hasn't been gone long enough, she had better wait. Besides, she knows that Robert would call her if he can, he probably can't because he is tied up, or isn't able to get to a phone. That's it, so she'd better stop worrying, he could come home at any moment.

It was now one in the afternoon on Monday, two days have gone by and still no word from Robert. Aunt Bea is beside herself. She is sure that something terrible must have happened to Robert. She calls the North Hollywood Police station and talks to Detective Tony Milano of the missing person's section, she gives him the facts. Milano is a veteran cop in his forties, a big good-looking man with deep piercing hazel eyes that could make anyone a little uneasy if they were lying, or hiding any information from him.

The detective, had heard Beatrice Turner's story thousands of times about a family member who is missing. He investigated many endless cases. He found that ninety percent of those who were missing didn't meet with foul play, but were just off on an extended week end, or just shacking up, or searching to find another life for themselves somewhere else. However, in Aunt Bea's case, he was impressed with her story and agreed that something, or someone, must have caused her nephew's sudden disappearance on the night of the party.

Aunt Bea sits in a chair facing Detective Milano, who is sitting behind his desk in the North Hollywood Police Station. Milano is writing some notes on a pad, he finishes his writing and then looks up at Aunt Bea. "Ms. Turner, I will investigate your nephew's disappear-ance immediately," says Milano. "Oh thank you Detective Milano. God bless you," says Aunt Bea holding back her tears.

"Don't thank me, ma'am, it's my job. I do believe something has happened to your nephew," says Milano with a sympathetic tone in his voice.

Aunt Bea leaves the North Hollywood Police Station and Detective Milano starts the machinery in motion. He puts out a missing persons APB using one of Robert's theatrical pictures, that aunt Bea gave him. Then he calls the Canin's and tells them he that he is investigating Robert Anthony's disappearance and he wants to see them as soon as possible, like tomorrow. Aunt Bea is sitting on her couch in a daze and her only thoughts are of her nephew Robert. Her eyes begin to fill with tears, and she cries out, "Oh, Robert, where are you." A flood of tears roll down her pale, gaunt, anguished face. "Oh God, please don't let anything happen to Robert." she prays.

Sam sees Aunt Bea crying and his animal instinct tells him that something must have happened to his master because he has not seen him around in the last few days. So he moves to Aunt Bea and he puts his head in her lap and begins to wail.

Chapter Six
Missing Person's
The Investigation

Joe and Ellen are seated on the couch in the large living room where the party was held. Detective Milano is sitting in an arm chair facing them. He shows a picture of Anthony to Joe Canin. Canin carefully studies Robert's photograph. After a long moment he looks up from Anthony's photo to Milano.

"He doesn't look like anyone I know who was invited to my party, I've never seen this man before, or know his name," insists Canin, handing back Robert's picture, to the cop.

"I see, but according to his aunt, Mr. Canin, she told me that he was invited," says Milano firmly.

"Well, maybe he got on my guest list without my knowledge," answers Canin honestly.

Milano sees that Ellen Canin is a little tense. "What about you Mrs. Canin?" handing her Robert's picture. "Did you see Robert Anthony at your party last Saturday night?" says the cop in a friendly tone of voice.

Ellen hesitates a moment. Then in a low, nervous breathy low whisper says, "Yes I did."

Milano, didn't quite hear what Ellen had just said, but her husband Joe did and he has a surprised look on his face. Canin turns to his wife and is about to say something to her, but the experienced detective beats him to the punch. "What did you say, Mrs. Canin?" asks Milano. "Excuse me, I didn't quite hear what you said."

Ellen clears her throat and takes a deep breath, "I'm so sorry, Detective Milano. What I said was, yes I did," says Ellen loud and clear. "Mr. Anthony did attend our Saturday night party." Milano smiles and nods his head. "Thank you, Mrs. Canin."

"Ellen, how did Anthony get on our guest list?" questions Joe, a little perturbed.

The big cop leans back into his chair, crosses his legs and waits to hear the true confessions from the Canin's.

"I put him on the list," confesses Ellen fearlessly. "Because Diana Stuart, called me. She told me that Harry was using Mr. Anthony in a big part in a film he was going to make in Montana and she asked me if I could invite him to the party so that he could meet the important Hollywood people we had invited and maybe that could help Mr. Anthony's career and Harry's movie," says Ellen smiling broadly covering up her tall story. She then looks deep into her husbands eyes and says in a sweet, "Don't fuck with me," tone of voice. "Joe, Harry and Ellen are our good friends, I wanted to do them a favor and I knew you would approve."

Joe gives Ellen a, 'I know you got me by the long and short hairs on my ass and balls grin'. "Of course I would have approved, my sweet. Harry is a very good friend of mine and you and Diana are very close. You had every right to help them," says Joe giving his wife a saccharin kiss on her cheek.

Milano is a damn good detective. He is very sharp and has a great instinct. He knows that the Canin's are playing 'a fuck you game' with each other. But he also knows that they are telling the truth, that they didn't know about Anthony's disappearance.

Milano thinks for a moment, then asks Ellen, "The time you saw Mr. Anthony, was he with someone?"

"Well, you see, I was escorting Sheik Seid's daughter. I mean the Sheik's future wife to meet our friends, when I ran into Diana and Harry."

"That's the Stuart's," says Milano knowingly.

"Yes, say the Stuart's. Anyway, they were with this very good-looking young man."

"Mr. Anthony, right?" confirms Milano.

"Yes. They introduced me to him and I in turn introduced them to Jasmine, the Sheik's lady."

"Is that right, then that was the first time you had ever laid eyes on Mr. Anthony," questioned the detective.

"Yes, the first time," answered Mrs. Canin.

"Mmm, ah, was there anyone else with the Stuart's?" continued Milano.

"No, except the Sheik's bodyguard was there, he watched over Jasmine," added Mrs. Canin. Milano nods his head in the affirmative. "Good. Mrs. Canin, did you see Mr. Anthony leave the party that night?" inquires Detective Milano casually.

"No," says Ellen. "As a matter of fact on Sunday afternoon I went to an auction sale in Beverly Hills. My Chauffeur informed me that our garage attendant told him that there was one car left in the guest parking area from the Saturday night party. It was a 1992 silver Toyota. He checked the car registration to see who it belonged to and it was Robert Anthony's and,"

Milano quickly cuts Ellen off. "Why didn't you tell me this before Mrs. Canin?" says Milano annoyed.

"Well I didn't think about it till now. I've never been questioned by a policeman before. I'm a little nervous," says   Ellen with honest intention.

WILLIAM HELLINGER

The detective thinks a moment. "That's understandable," smiles Milano. Ellen returns her understanding smile.

Joe gives his wife a long stare. "Ellen, why didn't you tell me that one of our guests left his car in the parking area," says Joe perturbed.

"Well, I didn't think it was that important because I figured he would pick up the car eventually," says Ellen truthfully.

Milano jumps right in. "Where did you think Mr. Anthony was, Mrs. Canin?" chimes Milano.

Ellen quickly answers the cop without hesitation. "Well, I assumed that he must have left the party with a lady."

"What made you assume that, Mrs. Canin?," pipes Milano.

Ellen glances at her husband for a moment and smiles confidently. "Diana, Mrs. Stuart told me, that women were drawn to Mr. Anthony. That's why I thought nothing of Mr. Anthony's car still being there," answers Ellen shooting a look to Joe.

Joe glares at his wife. "Is that right, Ellen? Detective Milano, what my wife is trying to say is that Mr. Anthony is a Hollywood stud," says Canin laughing.

"Is that right, Mr. Canin. You know I'm really not interested in Mr. Anthony's politics. I'm only interested in finding out where he is, okay?" says the cop very annoyed.

"Sure, of course I understand," replies Joe with a half smile on his lips. It is his way of apologizing to Milano because he doesn't want to say he was sorry for what he had said. Milano gives him a quick look and then gets to his feet. "Well, Mrs. Canin, from all that you were able to tell me and other information from Mr. Anthony's aunt, I think that something foul has occurred to Mr. Anthony," declares the veteran lawman pulling no punches.

"Oh my God," gasps Ellen.

"That's too bad," says Joe not being to sympathetic.

"Yes, it doesn't look too good, but me and my department will do everything possible to find Mr. Anthony, dead or alive," says Milano with definite assurance. "But, if we hit a concrete wall, then, Mr. Anthony will be just another missing person statistic," says the big cop sadly. "I want to thank you both for your cooperation."

Joe and Ellen give Milano a 'you're welcome' smile and get to their feet.

"Well, in the meanwhile if either of you hear anything regarding Mr. Anthony's whereabouts, I would appreciate you getting in touch with me," mentions the detective.

"We'll do that," says Canin.

"Absolutely Detective, Milano. I'll keep my eyes and ears open. Oh, that poor Mr. Anthony, he looked like a nice young man", says Ellen meaning it. She then turns to her husband. "You would have liked his looks, Joe. Diana and Harry couldn't say enough about him. You would probably have used him in one of your films," says Ellen giving her husband a knowing smile.

Joe got Ellen's message and smiled broadly. "Yes, probably, it's just too bad honey that I might never get the opportunity to have him in one of my movies," says Canin with a false remorse.

"Well, you have my card," says the cop. "If either of you hear of anything, or think of something that you might have forgotten to tell me, give me a call, okay?"

The Canin's simultaneously nodded their heads and smile." Oh, you can count on us," says Joe with assurance.

"Again, thanks for your cooperation," says Milano. He steps away from them and starts out of the room. The smiling couple watch the cop disappear into the foyer. Joe turns to Ellen and is about to say something to her, when suddenly Milano, reappears in the archway. "Oh, I'll be notifying the police garage to pick up Mr. Anthony's car. We'll have it dusted and go over it with a fine tooth-comb for any clues that might help us find him," states the detective. Then he turns and disappears into the foyer.

Joe and Ellen stand there without saying a word to each other. After a couple of moments they hear the front door open and then close. "I do hope that Detective Milano is wrong about Mr. Anthony meeting with foul play," says Ellen with a genuine concern.

"If anything did happen to him, I just hope the hell that it wasn't any of my guests or friends wife's or daughter's, who left with Mr. Anthony that night," declares Joe, with great seriousness. "Well, I got a production meeting this afternoon. Sorry about your loss and Diana's, don't wait up for me," says Joe and quickly leaves the room. She stares after her husband. "Joe Canin, you're an unfeeling bastard."

Ellen is very disturbed about Robert's disappearance though she really didn't know him. She knew about Robert from what Diana told her about him. When she did meet him she thought he seemed like a nice person, very sensual, exciting, very good looking, sexy. Alas, she will never have those wonderful, countless orgasms Robert had given to her sex starved girl friend, Diana. Ellen sighs sadly, drops down on the couch and thinks for a moment. Then she picks up the cordless phone from the coffee table, stretches her body out on the couch, props her head on a pillow and then in a prone position punches in a hone number on the cordless and waits. After a beat, she hears phone on the other end start ringing and on the fourth ring, a female voice answers, "Hello?" Ellen smiles and replies, "Diana Ellen here."

"Oh hi, what's going on?" requests Diana.

Ellen doesn't mince any words and gets to the core of her bad tidings. "Diana, something terrible has happened to Robert Anthony," says Ellen with regret.

"What was that." says Diana shocked.

"I said," Ellen couldn't finish her sentence because Diana jumps in quickly and cuts her off.

"Ellen, I heard what you said, what's happened to Robert?"

"He's been missing since the night of the party. His Aunt called the police on Monday and reported him missing."

"Oh my God, that's why he didn't keep his appointment with Harry. Harry thought that Robert forgot his meeting with him, or was to busy fucking some producer's wife. He figured, Robert would call him in a few days to pick up the script. Boy was Harry wrong, I felt something wasn't right. He would have called me if he couldn't make his appointment. Robert wanted that part in Harry's movie, so badly," replies Diana puzzled.

"Well, that isn't all. A Detective Milano from missing person's was here today questioning me and Joe. He thinks that Robert has met with foul play," Ellen relates.

There is a deep pause. "Ellen, I just can't believe that anyone would hurt Robert. I didn't know him that well, but from what I saw of him and what he said to me, he seemed like a good guy. Why would anyone want to hurt him?" laments Diana.

"Who knows Diana," answers Ellen. "Maybe, he was waylaid by a jealous husband," says Ellen with a foreboding tone of murder.

Chapter Seven
Detective Milano's Report

Robert's silver Toyota had revealed nothing that would indicate what had happen to Robert. For almost eight months Detective Milano conducted a thorough investigation. His depart-ment in conjunction with other states and national bureau's all came up with zero. Robert Anthony was assumed dead.

Milano reported the findings to Beatrice Turner, she was heart-broken. He wanted to console her, but the detective felt it would be better to let her cry it out. Even Sam lying at Aunt Bea's feet must have known why she was crying and he wailed softly with her. Beatrice Turner's tears subsided and Sam's wailing did too. Aunt Bea's eyes were red and her face was pale and gaunt.

Milano took her hand to comfort her. "M's. Turner, I want you to know that I will keep Robert's missing persons file open, until there is a resolution. I will make sure that it's not closed." He tries to give Aunt Bea a ray of hope.

Aunt Bea's lips, slowly form a little smile and says, "Detective Milano, I really appreciate all that you've done for me. With the help of the police department I know that Robert will be found alive, I can feel it in these old bones of mine. Every tingling nerve in my body is telling me Robert's is alive and that he can't contact me to say he's alright," says Aunt Bea with lots of faith, courage and hope.

"You're right, I have almost the same feeling that he may be out there somewhere, not able to make his way back," states Milano who Aunt Bea believes in.

"You know, I never called Blockmasters, that's the place he worked at, I should tell them what's happened to Robert."

Milano is puzzled with Aunt Bea's statement. "Ms Turner, didn't you know that your nephew stopped working at Blockmasters?"

"That can't be," says Bea puzzled.

"That's what they had told me. They said he left there over a year ago to work as a stripper at Mahoganys' in Beverly Hills," answers Milano.

"But it can't be. Robert wouldn't do that without telling me," says Aunt Bea a little hurt.

"Maybe he wanted to make more money. The manager at Mahoganys' told me that he was their best stripper. It paid very well." quotes Milano.

Aunt Bea thinks for a moment. Robert must have found out that she was in need of money to pay her bills and that's why he took the job at Mahoganys'. That's why he said that Blockmasters' had given him a raise, he didn't want her to know that he went to work as a stripper.

"Robert was a good boy, Detective Milano. He just changed his job to make more money for us that's all," says Bea defending her nephew's new occupation as a stripper.

"Nothing wrong with that," says the understanding cop. "Well, Ms. Turner, I will keep in touch with you, if there is any news about Robert."

"Thank you again, for all your help and for being so understanding," says Aunt Bea.

The detective leaves the house with Aunt Bea looking out the window watching Milano's car drive off and disappear round the corner of the street. She reaches down to Sam and strokes his head. "Sam, I know we'll see Robert again."

Sam answers aunt Bea with a loud bark.

Chapter Eight
Harut City, Bokuf
Eight months later

Oil wells are visible as far as the eye can see. They cover the desert ground that surrounds the small Arab City of Bokuf. The flames and smoke that come from the derricks show it is very rich in oil productivity. Many of the modern paved roads that skirt and run through the oil fields come into this city. The highways give the citizens of Bokuf a better access to the capital.

From the top of the cities tallest modern skyscraper, Sheik Seid's Palace can be seen west of the city. A TV satellite dish sits on top of the Sheik's domed roof building, the dish receives television programs from all over the world.

Anyone approaching the Palace is stopped by a twelve foot high beautiful multi-colored, thick tile and brick wall, that surrounds the ancient facility. The only way into the Palace grounds is through high thick oak doors that are closed at all times. The big doors are operated by a computer that opens and closes with the password of "Open Sesame." Only special people have that code to enter, while others must press an electronic communicator to announce themselves in order for entry to the Palace.

Abdullah is standing guard at the door of Sheik Seid's study. He stands there erect, arms folded, eyes straight ahead, there is no emotion registered on his big face. He doesn't move a muscle, making him look

WILLIAM HELLINGER

more like a statue dressed in Arabian clothes with a sword attached to his waist.

Sheik Seid is in his spacious study seated behind his large desk that is equipped with an electronic communication system. This sophisticated unit can contact anyone in all the corners of the globe. The Sheik uses this as his office and meeting room. The expensive furniture includes a 60 inch TV set all in a modern Eastern motif. The rest of the furnishings throughout the building are also in the same design, except for the rugs on the Palace floors which are old and very beautiful.

Seated around the Sheik's desk are three Arab women Ayesha, pretty in her thirties. Sukayna, very lovely, in her twenties. The last is Aida who is just turning twenty, extremely attractive and shapely. All of them are dressed in the finest custom made Arabic clothes. All of these woman have the same thing in common, they are three of the Sheik's eight Harem wives. The Sheik purchased them, or they were given to him as a gift from their families.

All of Sheik Seid's wives, speak and understand English. He makes them watch American and English television programs that are transmitted to their satellite dish, on to their large TV screens. The Sheik's motive was that he conducted all of his business in the world markets, where only English is spoken.

The Harem women love the English language because they can especially watch the American soap operas.

The Sheik is happy he smiles broadly as he surveys his lovely brood of young wives. The smiling ladies rise from their chairs, "Good morning my husband the Sheik," declare the elated Harem women all in unison.

"Good morning, my precious wives," recants the Sheik. He leans back in his chair and cups his hands together. "Now, for your report, Ayesha," commands the Sheik.

Ayesha quickly punches up some figures on her lap—top computer. She finishes with her computations and reads them off. "One hundred tons of dates were harvested last month and exported to the Arab-American Date Corporation. A payment of four hundred thousand dollars was credited to your Swiss account," Ayesha is very happy to inform her husband, the Sheik. Then says, "I am on the ball, yes, my husband?"

"Yes, you are. It is excellent, Ayesha. You have gotten twenty five percent more on this date crop. How did you do that?" says the Sheik with a happy smile on his face.

"My Sheik, I investigated the date retail prices around the world. The health markets in America are the highest, so I knew they would pay the increase, supply and demand," says Ayesha smiling proudly.

"Stupid Americans," declares the Sheik laughing loudly at what his cunning wife had done. Then Ayesha joins in on her husbands laughter, as does Aida and Sukayna.

When the Sheik stops laughing, so do his three wives. Ayesha continues her report. "My husband, tomorrow I will send the Prime Minister the annual report on Bokuf's oil production." She leans over to Seid, and whispers to him, "Of course, the figures will not reflect, four million dollars, that I deposited in your secret Curacao account," says Ayesha winking and smiling proudly to her Sheik.

The Sheik is extremely elated. "Yes, that makes me very happy. I am very proud of you, Ayesha," says the Sheik winking back at her. Then he claps his hands. "My wives, you may all leave now," he says as he gets up from his chair. "I will see you all at supper tonight."

"We all can not wait my husband," reply his three smiling wives. The three women get to their feet and form a line. Then one by one, they kiss their lord and master on the cheek and start to leave the room.

"Oh, Aida," says the Sheik stopping the three women at the door.

Aida turns to the Sheik. "Yes, my Sheik."

"Aida, before we eat, you and I will play some water games in the pool," says the grinning dirty old Sheik as he rubs his hands together sensually.

Aida Chuckles knowingly. Ayesha and Sukayna laugh and make delightful sounds of Aida's before dinner sexual encounter. The women

WILLIAM HELLINGER

leave the room laughing and the Sheik can still hear his wives laughter echoing and fading away, as they move down the Palace corridor.

The Sheik feels good, he thought a lot about his young wives, how smart and obedient they all were. They would do anything for him, because they all loved him very much. And sex with all of them was great, he taught them well also.

Sheik Seid knew that most of the Sheik's in Bokuf were having problems with their Harems, so he was truly a lucky man. He sighs gratefully, expands his loyal chest with great pride, then follows that with a smile as large as the room he was in. The Sheik is very happy and quite content. He knows he has everything a man could wish for, wealth, power and sex to get laid anytime he wanted to. He chuckles, looks up to Allah, to thank him, his father and the long line of the royal Seid clan.

Smiling, he sits back down at his desk, leans back in his chair and closes his eyes. He is proud of his accomplishments, he idolizes himself. He sits there for a few moments when a thought strikes him. He leans forward and hits the intercom button on his desk.

Immediately a male voice with a refined Arab, English accent, comes out of the speaker. "My Sheik," declares the voice.

"Doctor Kalila," says Seid.

"Yes, Ali," replies Doctor Kalila.

"Rashid, do you think we can awake our guest?" questions the Sheik. "I do not see why we can not," agrees the doctor.

Seid smiles with satisfaction. "Good, Rashid, do it now," says the Sheik emphatically. He switches off the intercom, leans back in his chair and lets out a pleasing laugh.

The door to Doctor Kalila's office in Sheik Seid's Palace swings open. Doctor Kalila a dark, pleasant looking man of fifty, comes out of the room. He is followed by his assistant, Doctor Dimna Gailm, a lean, thirty five year old Arab, who is carrying a black medical bag. The two men move down the Palace corridor until they come to a stairway that goes down to the Palace dungeon. Both doctor's, walk quickly down

THE FIRST LADY

the brightly lit dungeon hallways that crisscross the bottom floor of the building. The dungeon has been remodeled to reflect modern times. Its walls were covered with blue and orange colored tiles. Flanking both sides of the pathway are oak panel doors, where there use to be cell doors .The dungeon is no longer used as a torture killing den or prison for Sheik Seid's enemies. The once ominous, depressing place now has a cheerful appearance. Since the rich oil discovery in Bokuf, unrest and dissent had disappeared.

The doctors round a bend in the corridor and go down the long hallway. At the far end of corridor is a guard on duty, who stands against an oak door. His left eye is covered with a black eye patch and on the left side of his cheek there is a long ugly jagged scar that ends at his jaw, the guard is Karim. Doctor Kalila and his assistant approach the big man at the door. Karim sees them, he moves away from his post and opens the door for them. Doctor Kalila nods his 'thank you' to Karim and the two doctors enter the room. Karim closes the door and dutifully takes up his position again.

The gigantic bedroom, is immaculately designed and furnished. On the upper left side of the room there is a bathing area with an Italian marble floor. It surrounds a large tile sunken tub 4 foot deep by ten foot long. There is a long, white marble bench, at the upper edge. The different colored lights around the room are softly lit and gives the room an erotic look. One would never guess that this room had been a torture chamber.

Kawakib is an elderly Arab female nurse who is wearing a gray nurse's uniform. She stands at the foot of a much larger than king sized bed. The large bed has been customized into a hospital bed and has a fluffy canopy over it. Pink colored silk 'see-thru' drapes hang from a canopy. It covers all sides of the bed, from the top, to its bottom. A reclining form can be seen on the bed though the pink drapes.

"Good morning, Doctor Kalila, Doctor Gailim," says the nurse who can only speak and understand Arabic.

"Good morning, Nurse Kawaib," responds both doctors. Doctor Kalila moves to the bed and observes the sleeping figure for a moment. "How is my patient?" asks the doctor.

"She is stable, doctor," answers the nurse.

"Good. It's time for me to awaken her, prepare her," declares Doctor Kalila.

The doctor's command propels the elderly nurse into action. She grabs the bed controls at the front of the bed and pushes one of the remote buttons. There is a humming sound, after a few moments the humming stops. She quickly pulls aside the beds silk coverings, revealing a beautiful young woman. Her upper body is in a raised position. Her long flowing red hair is spread on the pillow framing her face. The silk blue of the colored pillow case in contrast makes her hair look as though it was on fire. The blue covers are rolled down to her waist, exposing the curvature of her beautiful body and large, lovely shaped breasts barely covered by a low-cut, black negligee. And with each breath she takes, her breasts rise and fall.

Two I.V. bags hang on a hooks attached to the bed's canopy. One bag contains saline and drains down into her arm from a tube that is injected intravenously into her right wrist. The other bag is filled with a life sustaining food source Ensure, that is attached to another tube that leads into the sleeping beauty's stomach.

Nurse Kawakib rolls a cart full of medical supplies that she has taken from the medical cabinet over to the patient's bed side. Both doctor's remove their jackets and join the 'Angel of Mercy'. The elderly nurse then places surgical gloves, on to each Doctor's, extended hands.

Kalila leans over his patient, observes the beautiful woman for a moment and smiles broadly. He then reaches for the saline needle in her arm and removes it. He waits for a reaction from the lady, but there is none. He nods to his nurse, who then lowers the silk covers down to the redhead's knees. This action reveals the entry of the Ensure's feeding tube, which had been injected into the beauty's stomach and a catheter which had been inserted into the woman's urethra. There is a draining tube leading into a half filled bag of liquid. It hangs over the foot of the bed. Doctor Kalila removes the draining tube and he passes it to the nurse, who disposes it.

Doctor Kalila stares intently at the lovely woman's vagina and smiles happily from ear to ear. With anxious anticipation, Doctor Gailam his assistant, leans over and watches Kalila give a full examination of the

THE FIRST LADY

gorgeous girl's 'love nest'. Gailam smiles with great satisfaction. The face of the elderly nurse is completely expressionless.

Doctor Kalila then examines the feeding tube. The skillful doctor carefully removes the tubing out of the young girls stomach along with the dressing that surrounds it. The nurse hands Doctor Gailam cotton swabs and the doctor mops up the area, cleaning it thoroughly with this antiseptic spray. The nurse then gives Doctor Kalila a threaded surgical needle. The doctor sutures the small opening where he had removed the feeding tube. Doctor Gailam applies an antibiotic cream and bandage to complete the procedure.

Doctor Kalila nods to his nurse. She pulls the covers back up to the redhead's waist. Nurse Kawakib then picks up a hypodermic packet and a caddy from the cart. She takes out one of the small bottles from the caddy, which was filled with a white liquid substance, then tears open the hypodermic packet and pulls out one of the syringes. She pulls the needle guard off the hypodermic, sticks the needle into the vial and sucks up some of the fluid. She hands the full hypodermic syringe to Doctor Kalila. He picks up the woman's right arm, plunges the needle into her vein and empties the contents of the syringe into it. The two medico's, focus on the redhead and wait, with great anticipation for the drug to take its effect.

Moments go by and the beautiful woman begins to stir. Her lips move and her head rolls back and forth on the pillow, followed by several small moaning sounds that come out of her throat. The two men smile. The elderly nurse is unmoved, she just observes the patient's awakening.

The redhead's eyes start to flutter, then they flip open. She tries to raise her head, but it flops back on to the pillow, her eyes roll around in her head. She is trying to focus. When she does, she stares up and sees the life support bags that hang over her. A long loud, frightening scream comes out of her mouth. The doctor's, are not surprised by the woman's reaction. But the redhead shocks herself by the high shrill piercing sound of her scream.

Her upper body springs up, with her hands covering her mouth. She is frozen, silent, confused, disoriented. She takes several deep breaths and her mouth begins to form a word, but no words come out. She tries to speak again, and this time only garbled sounds come out of her mouth. She is shocked and puzzled, as she tries to gather her wits and she waits a moment. Then suddenly, she screams gruffly at the top of her lungs, "What, the fuck is going on. Where, the hell am I, I feel strange. Oooha, Oooha my head. Dizzy."

The redhead looks around at her strange unfamiliar surroundings. Her eyes catch Doctor Kalila who is proudly smiling and Doctor Gailam who is wide-eyed and grinning. The elderly nurse remains dead-panned.

Doctor Kalila knew how his patient would react. With a bedside manner he takes her hand gently to calm her. "I know you are disoriented, but that will soon pass," says Doctor Kalila with a soft smile.

The redhead's eyes keep scanning the three strange people who are looking down at her. She tries to regain her recall, but at the moment she can't.

Kalila waits patiently for the women to come out of her confused and depressed state of mind.

The redhead stares at the doctor for several moments, trying to regain her thoughts. After a moment, her wild look and puzzlement disappear from her eyes. Calmly, softly, "Where, am," she starts to say, but she stops speaking when she hears this sultry voice coming out of her own mouth. She shakes her head to clear it, still trying to remember something, but just can't. She looks intently at the three strangers for their help. The doctor's, give the redhead an encouraging smile. The nurse's face is bland, unmoved.

The beautiful woman's eyes shift from side to side, then stops and a determined look comes over her face. Her hand moves to the covers and pushes them aside. She pivots herself slowly to the edge of the bed, sitting there with her feet touching the floor. The doctors observe her, with broad smiles of anticipation. After a few unsteady moments she tries to get to her feet. When she does she winces and feels a slight pain that comes from her stomach. She drops back down on the bed in a sitting position. The doctor's are not to be surprised by the discomfort and pain of getting on her feet.

She touches her stomach where her pain is coming from and is shocked to feel a bandage underneath the silky material she is wearing. The touch of the silky cloth on her body confuses her. She looks down at her body and sees she is wearing a revealing black negligee. Her eyes widen in horror, confusion and puzzlement. The beautiful redhead lets out a blood-curdling scream. She tries to get to her feet again and does. But her legs gave way. She falls to the floor in a sitting position, with her back resting against the bed.

The nurse moves quickly to the far end of the room retrieving a wheel chair and pushes it to the confused woman. The two doctors help the woman into the chair. Then Kalila sits down at the edge of the bed facing the dazed lady. He looks at her with comforting smiling eyes.

It doesn't take too long before the beautiful redhead calms down. She is bewildered and stares questionably at Doctor Kalila who is smiling at her.

"Who the fuck are you?" shouts the bewildered women.

"I am Doctor Rashid Kalila," says the smiling doctor in a calm friendly tone of voice.

"Doctor?" the puzzled redhead screams. She looks around the room. "What the hell is this place?" asks the confused women.

"You are in the Palace of Sheik Ali Seid, oil minister of Bokuf," says Doctor Kalila in a tours guide tone of voice.

"Sheik Seid, Bokuf?" says the redhead shocked, puzzled and confused. "Sheik Seid? Sheik Seid? Sheik Seid?" she repeats, trying to remember who Seid is but can't. She becomes panicky. "What the fuck am I doing here? What the fuck is going on?" she declares screaming in Kalila's face.

Her outburst doesn't phase Doctor Kalila. He just smiles. The redhead takes a deep breath, it calms her down. Again she surveys her body. Still confused she can't even fathom what was going on, she closes her eyes tightly, shakes her head slowly, trying to remove the cobwebs in her head. She flips her eyes open then she looks around the room observing everything in it. Her eyes focus on Doctor Kalila's smiling face. She grabs the handles of the wheel chair and pushes herself up to her feet, she is a little wobbly. She moves to the back of the chair and grips the top of it to help her stand up. She leans into Kalila's face. "Doctor," pleading, then angry. "What the fuck have you done to me Doctor?" shouts the beautiful woman.

Doctor Kalila waits for the women to settle down for this big announcement. "Robert Anthony, you have been transformed into a transsexual," answers the doctor in a professional manner.

"What? What the fuck are you talking about," shouts Anthony with disbelief.

"That you have been turned into a woman. A beautiful, shapely female, undetectable in every way," states Doctor Kalila matter-of-factly.

"You're full of fucking shit, Doc. I don't believe you," says Anthony laughing incredulously in the doctor's face. Doctor Kalila is now a little impatient. He shakes his head at Anthony for her insistent denial and disbelief. "Oh, yes Ms. Anthony. You are a lady now and there is no one that could ever tell that you were once a man," says the doctor with professional glee about Anthony's sex change.

The beautiful redhead's shocked mind explodes as though it was hit by a hydrogen bomb. Anthony throws her head back and lets out a long mournful wail. Her mind starts to clear as realization begins to set in. "A transsexual, a woman," says Anthony with a sinking feeling.

"Yes," says the doctor happily. "I assisted Doctor Girard Faux of Paris France. He is the finest transsexual surgeon in the world. At first Doctor Faux refused to do the illegal transformation on you, but then Sheik Seid offered him a small fortune. The fee was fine, but only on one condition, that he would perform a new surgical technique he had just developed in transsexual transformations. You have been here asleep now eight months. We treated you with every kind of hormone and drug to make you perfect and you are perfect. Just perfect in every way," confesses Doctor Kalila smiling proudly for his part in Anthony's new female identity.

Anthony moans with anguish. Her eyes focus on a large full length mirror that hangs on the wall in the bathing area. Anthony steps away from the chair and struggles to her feet to get to the mirror.

The three Arabs observe the beautiful transsexual as she moves painfully across the room. They wonder what her destination is until she gets to the mirror on the wall and stands very close to it looking at the imaged reflection.

Now Doctor Kalila realizes why Anthony is at the mirror. So he continues to inform Anthony about the operation that changed his gender. "Doctor Faux, even gave you a beautiful nose and reshaped your eyes to make your new change complete. That was his idea. The man is an artist, a genius," declares Doctor Kalila with his worshiped testimony of the man who recreated Anthony.

Anthony stared into the mirror nervously. She examines her nose, eyes, face, long red hair and carefully explores her new body. She roams from her lovely breasts to her buttocks.

The two doctors observe Anthony with sheer fascination. The elderly nurse looks at her with disdain, as a freak. Anthony slowly lifts up her negligee to her crotch. With increased fear she moves her hands down to that area, but hesitates a moment short of her target. Anthony takes a deep breath and continues to slide her hands down until she gets between her legs. She begins to investigate her private parts. Her eyes widen with stunned horror when she feels no penis. She quickly explores further. Her hand stops when she reaches a slit below, where the penis use to be. Her forefinger slides inside the grove between her legs and probes it from its top, its bottom and its depth. She gets a sinking feeling in her stomach because it feels exactly like a vagina. She now knows it is a vagina, just like other women have. Her heart begins to beat like the rapid fire of an AK 47.

Anthony's mouth forms the words, 'OH MY GOD'. 'I AM A WOMAN' and then lets out a scream that would have awakened all of the dead, in all of the Arab Republic cemeteries. It shocked Doctor Kalila and his assistant, Doctor Gailam. It even horrified the unfeeling nurse.

"You dirty son-of-bitches. You lousy mother-fucking bastards. I hope you, Sheik Seid and that rotten mother-fucking Doctor Faux, die horrible deaths and rot in hell," bellows Anthony in a lamenting, tearful wail. She turns away from the mirror. "I wish, I was dead," says Anthony sobbing.

Anthony wipes her wet eyes and tear-stained cheek with her arm. She stares directly into Doctor Kalila's eyes with anger and hate. "You call yourself a doctor, you're nothing but a miserable piece of shit. Why was this done to me? Why? Why?" shouts Anthony in a loud, sharp piercing cry.

Doctor Kalila says nothing. He does understand Anthony's horrifying discovery that he is not the man he once was. However, he did not give a Camels turd. Anthony got what he deserved and he had no pity for Anthony's misery. As a doctor he was very happy that he had participated in the historic event. He wanted to say, "But you are now a 'born again' beautiful woman. Then Doctor Kalila smiles to himself and thinks of what Allah would say about Anthony's conversion, "You cannot fuck with an Arab and expect to get away with it," unquote.

Anthony deeply depressed, staggers to the marble bench and sits down. She lowers her head and covers her face with the palm of her hands. "What did I do to deserve this. Why, why," whispers Anthony with anguish.

Doctor Kalila gets up from the edge of the bed and moves to the lamenting redhead. "Tomorrow you will meet with Sheik Seid and then you will know why," says the doctor in a professional tone of voice.

Doctor Kalila stares at the depressed, grief stricken woman. He takes a hypodermic out of the medication caddy. He slips off the needle guard and picks out a small vial of medication from it. He inserts the needle into the tube and sucks out some of the fluid into the hypodermic. He goes to Anthony, lifts up the right sleeve of her negligee and with no resistance from her he injects the liquid into a vein in her arm.

The tranquilizer immediately takes effect on Anthony. When the nurse puts her back into bed she falls into a deep sleep.

The next day, Sheik Seid sits in his arm chair behind the desk in his study. Anthony is seated in a chair facing him. She is dressed in a beautiful Arabian robe that compliments her red hair. Abdullah, the Sheik's guard stands at attention behind her chair. An evil, revengeful smile is on the Sheik's lips.

"You did this to me because I fucked Jasmine before you did," declares the shocked Anthony.

THE FIRST LADY

"Yes, in my country you committed a terrible crime," retorts the Sheik.

"Yeah, well in my country it's only a crime when she's under age and even then you're sent to jail with your manhood intact," says Anthony bitterly.

"Stupid Americans," says the Sheik laughing. "But it could have been worse for you, I could have cut your throat and fed your carcass to the crocodiles," says the Sheik calmly and smiling.

"You should have, you dirty scum bag prick," responds Anthony with a hate that could kill.

The Sheik laughs masochistically. "That would have been too merciful, you deserved much worse. Instead, I let the punishment fit the crime. I had your prick cut off, turned you into a transsexual who now looks like a very beautiful woman, I must say," says the Sheik with joyful revenge.

"Flattery will get you nowhere, you fuckin prick," says Anthony with dry anger.

"Ahh and with a woman's sense of humor too," says the Sheik with an ironical laugh. "Those special female hormones that Doctor Faux prescribed for you are really working perfectly Rob, Rob," says the Sheik hesitating. He thinks for a moment, then his face lights up and he smiles. "Yes, Roberta. Roberta is more correct for your new birth, Ms. Roberta Anthony. You had better play the role Anthony, if you want to survive in your new life," declares the vengeful Sheik.

Anthony's lips tighten, "Some day, you'll pay for what you've done to me and you will regret it," Anthony states firmly. "I will get even with you," he says seething.

Sheik Seid roars with a knowing laugh. "Roberta, where I am going to send you, you will be in no position to do anything to anyone, ever," says the Sheik in a calm, ominous tone of voice.

"Send me, where?" asks Anthony in a stunned surprised voice.

"To my good friend, Sheik Mohammed Kassem. You will be a gift for his Harem. That is the final part of your sentence." responds Sheik Seid in a sober, happy final act of his revenge.

"You crazy Arab bastard," yells the shocked Anthony.

"No, it is good diplomacy," states the Sheik laughing.

Anthony gives the Sheik an 'I've got you smile' and declares, "Oh yeah, not after I tell your friend who I was and what you've done to me."

Sheik Seid laughs his ass off. "Oh, Roberta, Mohammed does not care what you are, or who you were. He already knows what I done to you and he cannot wait to be with you on his honeymoon night. Oh, you will like my jolly fat friend," says the Sheik gloating.

"You dirty son-of-bitch. May your God, Allah damn your soul," says Anthony seething.

"If Allah were here he would approve of what I have done to you," says the Sheik with a pious look on his face.

"Then fuck him too," screams Anthony.

Sheik Seid's face hardens. "Enough talk. In a week you will be strong enough to leave for Sheik Kassem's Palace. I want you to be a lively, healthy plaything for my dear friend," says the Sheik sadistically. "Abdullah, take her back to her room," Seid orders his guard.

"Don't do this to me," says Anthony pleading quietly. But the Sheik is unmoved by Anthony's request. Seid gets up from his chair, moves to the door and turns to Anthony with a triumphant smile. "I am most happy and joyful of what I have done to you. I will be for the rest of my life, knowing that you will never fuck another women again," says the revenged Sheik with glee. "You're an inhuman sick fuckin' piece of shit." screams Anthony with hate.

Sheik Seid laughs tyrannically. With a cold tight lipped smile he turns to the door and leaves the room.

THE FIRST LADY

Anthony stares after him, her face reflects hopeless despair. Tears began to spill from her eyes down on to her beautiful face.

Chapter Nine
Hope is a Woman

Violet an Afro-American female Postal mail carrier in her late thirties inserts mail into Aunt Bea's next door neighbor's mail-box. Violet closes the box, adjusts her heavy loaded mail-bag and goes to Bea Turner's house. She walks to the front door and rings the door-bell. Violet's action has Sam barking from inside the house. It triggers barking of all the other dogs on the block. They give out the warning not to intrude on their territory. But Sam's bark is friendly, he likes Violet. He looks forward to seeing the mail-lady because she gives him his daily K-9 hello in cookies.

The front door opens and a warn looking Aunt Bea comes out. Sam follows her and he gives Violet a quick lick on her hand. Violet smiles and rubs Sam's head. The mail-lady then digs into her pocket pulls out a dog cookie and hold it up to her favorite dog. Sam quickly accepts Violet's daily offering, he loves her brand of cookies.

Sam chews the biscuit, swallows it, then moves to Aunt Bea and sits next to her. The dog pivots his head to both women, then cocks his ear and waits to listen to the two women's conversation. They think Sam understands everything they say, because during their chatter he would comment with a bark or a low grump. Sam was quite an animal.

Violet gives Aunt Bea a broad friendly smile. "Good morning Aunt Bea," says Violet in an upbeat voice as she hands her a few letters.

"Good morning Vi," says Bea in a tired voice as she takes the letters from her friend.

Violet sees that Bea is still, worn and worried. "Still no word from Robert?" asks Vi.

"No, Vi. And the police haven't come up with anything yet. But, I know when Robert's ready, he'll be in touch with me. I know he will," says Bea with moist eyes.

"Eight months without a word, terrible. You know some years ago I had a cousin who was missing for a year. They found him wandering the streets of St. Louis," Vi says in a consoling tone.

"Oh my God. Did the poor man lose his memory?" responds Aunt Bea.

"No," laughed Violet, "He was behind in his alimony. He owed his wife a ton of money, so he ran away."

"Robert is not married," says Aunt Bea who is puzzled by what the mail lady has said.

"I know, but he might owe a lot of money to a bookie," says Violet who really is serious.

"Robert doesn't gamble Vi, Robert is a good boy," Aunt Bea replies.

"I know, but I was just throwing out a possible reason for his disappearance. Bea, I do hope he contacts you, real soon," Violet says understandingly.

Aunt Bea forces a smile. She gives Violet a 'thank you' nod of her head. Violet gives her a quick hug and moves off down the street to deliver the rest of the mail. Sam barks a 'good-by bark.'

Tears are about to trickle down Aunt Beas cheeks. "Oh, Robert, where are you I know that you're alive, please come home," pleads Aunt Bea with tears streaming down her face.

THE FIRST LADY

When Sam sees that Aunt Bea is crying, he lets out a long, loud crying wail, then snuggles next to her.

Chapter Ten
A New Life For Roberta

Karim is standing guard at the front door of Roberta Anthony's room. He's standing at attention. His scared pale face is expressionless and his left eye is covered by a black patch. His thoughts are of his master Sheik Seid. He hates him for disfiguring his face and putting out his left eye. He knew it was his fault for not keeping guard of Jasmine at the Hollywood party. He always despised the Sheik for his cruelty to everyone in the Palace, even to his wives.

Then he had thought of what the Sheik had done to Anthony for taking Jasmine's virginity before he could. He turns this man into a woman for what he had done. He feels Sheik Seid committed a blasphemous act against Allah by turning Anthony into a female for that encounter against Allah. Allah, will be angry with Seid for breaking one of his ultimate laws, 'Born a man, die a man', 'Born a woman, die a woman.' Allah would have preferred, that Sheik Seid cut Anthony's head off as a fitting punishment for his deed against him and his Royal house.

Karim hoped that Allah would punish Seid very severely. But if Allah forgets to do that, Karim swears to Allah that he will get even with the Royal pig, someday.

The lights in Anthony's room are down low. The large tub is filled to the top with steaming vapors from the heat. Roberta is lying on the large bed. She wears a robe and she is staring up into the nowhere. Her face is sullen, her eyes are red, her cheeks are stained with tears. She is depressed, confused.

Then a thought hits her. What about my mind, I still have a brain. The brains of a man, now in the sensual body of a beautiful woman. How can I live as a woman who has the mind, of a man who could never keep his fly closed. A man who loved to be with woman and a man who used his sex drive to make it as an actor. Roberta was extremely confused for the only one thing she was sure of is that Robert Anthony's plans and future were now null and void.

Then Roberta's thoughts shifted to her Aunt Bea. Poor Aunt Bea what she must be going through with me missing all these months. She must be thinking that the baby she had raised, must be dead. If he wasn't, he surely would have contacted her. Poor Aunt Bea will never know what really happened to her Robert. Oh my God, she will die from a broken heart.

Tears come to Roberta's eyes. She gets up from the bed and sits at the edge of it. "I feel like I'm dead," she says to herself. "After today I'll be living in a Harem as one of the wives of a fat slob of a Sheik, who will have his way with me, any time and anyway he wants too. Will I live that way until the day I die. Nooo. I will not live that kind of life, I'd rather be dead." She wipes the tears away with the sleeve of her robe. "What the hell am I thinking, I could escape. Yeah. Escape from here, go to Paris, see Doctor Faux. Damn it. Force him to change me back to Robert Anthony. But I must find a way to get out of this Palace and be free." A sign of hope came over Roberta's face.

The door to Roberta's room swings open and a fat thirty eight year old Arab servant woman comes into the room. She is carrying a basin that contains a sponge, soap and shampoo. She is also holding a beautiful, colorful Arab cloth dress that hangs on a hanger. Draped over her arm are clean underwear and a large bath towel. She moves to the bathing area and sets her load down on the marble bench. Then she hangs the clothes up on a wall hook. She stares intensely at Roberta for a moment. In Arabic this large servant woman yells out, "All right lady. It is time for you to take your bath. You must be clean for your trip tonight. Now, come here."

Roberta doesn't move, she just sits on the bed. She doesn't understand what the woman is saying. But, she does know why the woman servant is there, so she just ignores her.

THE FIRST LADY

"Are you deaf, I said come here, you stupid American," screams the woman again in Arabic.

Roberta throws the woman an annoyed look and a go away motion with her hand. "Leave me alone, go away. I don't want you to give me any more baths," says Roberta knowing that the big woman doesn't understand English. She makes more hand signs to the woman indicating that she doesn't want her help and for her to leave the room.

The servant doesn't understand what Roberta is trying to tell her. She throws up her hands in disgust. The woman then signals to Roberta with her hands, to get into the tub.

Roberta knowing her protests would be to no avail, She gives up and throws up her hands in disgust and moves to her.

The servant tries to undress Anthony. Roberta shakes her head, 'no.' Then Roberta indicates that she can undress herself. The Arab woman loses all of her patience and screams a curse in her native tongue and starts to undress her. Roberta attempts to stop her and the two struggle. The woman accidentally slips and falls into tub. Her large body hits the bottom of the tub horizontally and what seems to be an eternity is just several seconds when Roberta sees that the big woman is lying at the bottom of the tub and not moving. She is about to jump into the three foot deep water to rescue the rotund servant, when the woman's head shoots to the surface of the water, bellowing angrily like a wounded whale. Roberta holds back a nervous laugh as she tries to help the Arab servant out of the tub, but the woman pushes her away screaming.

"You lousy fucking American freak, you tried to kill me. You dirty piece of Camel shit. I hope Allah sends you to hell, hell." says the water logged servant as she climbs out of the pool. The big woman stands there dripping wet glaring at Roberta with looks that could kill.

"I'm sorry that you fell into the tub, are you alright?" asks a concerned Roberta.

The servant is silent while several thin lines of water run down her angry face and eyes. She stares at Roberta for a moment and silently shuffles to the door and exits, leaving behind a trail of water on the exquisite expensive Arab rug.

Karim is still on guard at Roberta's bedroom door when the gross, water soaked woman goes past him. He is puzzled, even though he had heard the irate voice of the screaming servant. She was cursing Anthony in Arabic, which was echoing throughout the cellar corridors. When her voice diminishes to a silence, Karim shakes his head and shrugs.

Roberta is sitting on the bench by the tub, deep in thought contemplating her fate. With a forlorn look of hopelessness that appears on her beautiful face she thinks. How can I escape from here, it's impossible, it's guarded like Fort Knox. God please help me.

Getting to her feet, she slips off her robe and lets it fall on the bench. She then lowers herself into the tub and rests her head against the side of the pool. Starring up at the ceiling in thought her eyes become moist, but she slowly closes them tightly, to hold back her tears. She's resting there for several minutes when suddenly, she hears the sound of the bedroom door opening and closing. Roberta quickly opens her eyes, turns her head to the door and squints her eyes to see who had entered the room. A stunned look comes over her face as her eyes open wide.

Approaching her dressed in servants clothes and carrying a couple of bath towels, is the beautiful Jasmine. Anthony's face brightens when Jasmine approaches her. She smiles hopefully and holds up her face to the, lovely young girl. Jasmine doesn't recognize the transformed Robert and just gives Roberta a quick 'once over' look.

"I see you have undressed yourself," says Jasmine unmoved. "Sorry about the other lady, it was an accident," says Roberta with a big smile.

Jasmine still unmoved, starts to undress. "My name is Jasmine, I will bath you if that is alright," says Jasmine without any emotion.

"Yes, thank you Jasmine. You can scrub my back," says Roberta in a friendly manner.

Jasmine is taken aback by Roberta's cooperation. "Yes, you must be ready for your journey tonight," says Jasmine nicely. Roberta watches Jasmine take off the rest of her clothes until the shapely young girl is naked. Jasmine sees the basin, by the side of the tub and gets into the water.

THE FIRST LADY

Roberta turns her back and moves it close to Jasmine, who quickly works the soap into the sponge, then starts to wash Roberta's back very fast. When Jasmine finishes Anthony's smooth pretty back, she quickly washes other parts of the beautiful redhead's body. Throughout this hygienic action a silence prevails. But, when Jasmine starts to clean the lower front part of Roberta's body, this frustrates Roberta who then grabs Jasmine's arms, pushing her close to her breasts. This surprises and shocks Jasmine.

"What are you doing. Let me go. I do not make love with women," says Jasmine indignantly.

"I use to Jasmine, but not as I am," says Roberta quickly.

Jasmine is puzzled and tries to pull away from Roberta.

"Jasmine, listen to me, you know me," says Roberta softly.

"I do not know you, let me go," says Jasmine nervously. Roberta holds Jasmine tightly for an instant and then relaxes her grip to let her go. Jasmine moves to get out of the tub.

"Jasmine, please don't leave. You do know me, but not as I look to you now," says Roberta pleading.

Jasmine stops her escape, then she slowly turns to Roberta having a puzzled look on her face.

"Jasmine, look at me, into my face, my eyes, very deeply." Jasmine hesitates because she thinks that the beautiful redhead is playing for time to seduce her. But when she sees Roberta's lips form the word, "please," she looks into the girl's face intently. Jasmine strains to recollect and looks deeply into Roberta's beautiful face. Her eyes scans every angle of Roberta's face. But her recall is naught. "I am very sorry, I can not remember you," says Jasmine.

"Jasmine, I was hoping you would see some resemblance of my old self. Now listen, my change was very erratic." Jasmine's look was even more puzzled. "Okay! Jasmine, I'm the one you gave your virginity to," says Roberta factually.

Jasmine's body stiffens for a moment, then a long 'wail' comes out of her throat. She holds her head, shaking it from side to side as if she is going crazy. She tries to speak, but can't get a word out of her mouth.

Roberta sees the state Jasmine is in and she speaks very slowly, making sure that what she will now say will bring the young girl back from the state she was in. "Jasmine, I used to be, Robert. Robert Anthony," says Roberta with a soft smile.

Roberta's tenderness brings Jasmine back to her senses. "Robert. No. No. Oh my God, Allah," says the shocked Jasmine incredulously.

"Yes, it is me, Jasmine. The Sheik had me turned into a transsexual," explains Roberta as a forlorn conclusion.

Jasmine is completely stunned. She moves close to Roberta's face. She looks again. Now very deeply into Roberta's, pleading eyes. She holds her stare for a few moments, then Jasmine's face begins to brighten and cries out. "Oh, Allah be praised Robert, it is you! I thought that you were dead, that they had killed you that night." With extreme happiness, Jasmine wraps her arms tightly around Anthony.

Roberta sighs with relief and wraps her arms around Jasmine, even more tightly. "They did. Robert, is dead Jasmine," responds Roberta with finality.

"No. No. You are very much alive." They both sob together. "It is you with a new look. You were very handsome before, but now you are very beautiful with such perfect breasts," says Jasmine with extreme happiness, honesty and encouragement.

Roberta sighs as she looks at Jasmine's naked body. Roberta begins to laugh ironically, "No implants, hormones," but stops and quickly, but gently pushes Jasmine away from her body and tells her, "Allah, we'd better be careful, Sheik Seid might have me turned into a frog."

Jasmine thinks for a few seconds. Roberta's humorous joke has just struck her. She breaks out into hysterical laughter with Roberta joining in.

"A frog. Oh Robert," says Jasmine to Roberta laughing.

Roberta stops laughing. A serious look takes hold of her face and says, "Jasmine, due to my circumstances, call me Roberta for now."

"Yes, of course, Rob, Roberta," says Jasmine. The laughter continues.

Roberta smiles, and then the thought hits her. "Jasmine, how come the Sheik didn't get rid of you after what happened"'

"He did not want to send me back to my father, so he made me a servant. I work doing every kind of a menial job in the palace, from cleaning toilets to kitchen labor." Now Jasmine begins to cry as she continues to tell Roberta. "I am just a scullery maid, his prisoner. I will never get out of here, I am doomed for life. Oh Roberta," Jasmine is heartbroken.

"Yeah. Hey, look at me, I'm going to spend the rest of my life with a fat Sheik!" says Roberta as she ponders her thoughts. Jasmine starts to talk. "I know and it is all my fault that you are in this predicament." She wipes the tears from her eyes and face with her hand.

Roberta hasn't heard what Jasmine is saying, because she is turning something over in her mind. "Jasmine, we've got to find a way out of this mess."

"Escape?" says Jasmine understanding Roberta's statement.

"Yes, if that's possible," says Roberta positively.

"Maybe, but I do not know," says Jasmine dubiously.

"But we can try. I have nothing to lose," says Roberta encouragingly.

"Come to think of it, neither do I," says Jasmine.

"Are you sure, really sure?" asks Roberta. Jasmine nods her head 'yes' and smiles.

"Okay. Now tell me Jasmine, what time are they going to ship me out tonight and how?" Roberta begins to plot an escape.

Jasmine climbing out of the tub says to Roberta, "You are to leave at 8:P.M." Jasmine picks up a towel and begins to dry herself then continues, "You will be driven to the airport with a guard. Sheik Kassem's plane will be waiting to take you away," Jasmine gives Roberta her fateful itinerary, fact by fact. Roberta listens carefully while quickly boosting herself out of the tub. She picks up a towel and starts to dry her shapely body. Jasmine eyes her with an unbelieving look on her face.

"Jasmine, can you get a gun?" Roberta asks.

"I know where there is one, but I do not know if I can get it," Jasmine says quickly as she starts to dress.

"Where is the gun?" inquires Roberta.

"In the Sheik's bedroom. It is in the drawer of his night table, and I think that I may have a way to get the weapon," states Jasmine with a calculating half smile.

"All you can do is try, but, please be careful," Roberta replies concerningly as she puts on her dressing robe.

Jasmine is putting on the last of her clothes. "I will and if you don't see or hear from me." Her voice trails off.

Roberta in a tone of finality in her voice, "In that case, you'll know where I've gone."

They are both silent for a moment, as though they were praying to God for his help. Roberta breaks the silence. "Well, what happens next?"

Jasmine clears her throat. "At five they will bring you dinner. Then you will dress in those clothes," Jasmine points to the clothes on the wall hook.

"Then at seven thirty Abdullah will come for you. The rest you know. But if I am successful the rest will change."

"I hope so," Roberta sings out almost in prayer.

Jasmine's eyes are moist as she kisses Roberta on the cheek and moves to the door.

"Good luck, Jasmine," cries out Roberta.

Jasmine turns to Roberta with a soft smile. "Thank you Roberta, please say a prayer for us."

"You bet I will," answers Roberta.

Jasmine is about to open the door to leave, when Roberta cries out, "Oh, Jasmine."

Jasmine turns to Roberta, "Yes."

"I've been trying to figure out, how the Sheik got me out of America," Roberta wonderingly states.

"It had to be in the trunk of his Rolls Royce. Customs did not inspect the car when it boarded his jet, they never do. The Sheik has diplomatic immunity," answers Jasmine.

"That figures," says a sneering Roberta.

Jasmine smiles, opens the door and leaves the room.

Roberta stares after her with mixed emotions, of hope and doubt. God, please let Jasmine find that Arab bastards gun.

Chapter Eleven
Shipping Out

Lights are seeping through the many draped windows in Sheik Seid's Palace. A beautiful full-moon creates shadows and more light in the dark courtyard. The only sounds that are heard are coming from the yard. Two night birds are sitting together on the high surrounding wall chirping love calls to each other. The chirping is accompanied by a chorus of various types of desert insects sounds.

All these sounds stop abruptly when the courtyard lights are turned on. They light up the entire area. The two night birds are disturbed and fly off the wall to find another dark place to continue their chattering of love. While the bugs burrow under the sand and hide.

A white Rolls Royce makes its way from the rear of the courtyard and stops at the front door of the Palace. The chauffeur Kariff, is a lean thirty-five year old Arab. He is dressed in an Arab uniform and wearing brown leather gloves. His head is covered with a head cloth, which drapes on both sides of his face hiding it all except for a 'goatee' on his protruding chin. He watches closely as the front door of the Palace opens. Now his eyes focus on Roberta as slowly she comes out of the open door of the Palace and stops at the stairway. Abdullah is close behind her carrying a large suitcase. Then Kariff eyes Roberta's clothes. He sees that she is dressed in beautiful Arab clothes, with a colorful turban on her head that covers her flaming red hair. Make-up enhances her beauty. Kariff knows that Roberta's body has been oiled and perfumed for Sheik Kassem, because he can almost smell the scents. The chauffeur is very impressed with the way Roberta has been packaged.

Abdullah takes Roberta's arm and leads her down the steps carefully. When he reaches the courtyard, he guides her to the limousine. Abdullah opens the door of the Rolls Royce for Roberta and she and the chauffeur greet each other with the quick wave of a hand.

As Roberta is about to get into the limousine she freezes on the spot. She turns her head and looks in every direction of the courtyard to see if Jasmine is coming to her rescue. She sees nothing and she is frantic. After a few moments she realizes that Jasmine is not coming. The look of doom reflects in Roberta's face as she reluctantly gets into the vehicle.

Abdullah smiles when he closes the door of the big car behind Roberta. Then he moves with Roberta's suitcase to the rear of the Rolls and Kariff pops open the trunk. Abdullah places the bag into the trunk, closes it and goes to the front door of passenger side of the car and gets into the seat, leans back and folds his arms. Roberta sits in the corner of the big car, she appears beaten. Abdullah turns to Kariff and signals the man to go.

Kariff turns the motor on, puts the car into drive and the big car starts to move. Roberta begins to get panicky. "Stop." shouts Roberta. Roberta's command makes makes Kariff apply the brakes quickly bringing the Rolls Royce to a quick halt. Abdullah turns quickly to Roberta to Roberta. "What is wrong?" says the big body guard in broken English.

"I," says Roberta trying to stall as she glances through the car window to see if Jasmine was coming to storm the big white tank with a blazing gun. "I, forgot my make-up kit," says Roberta with a good excuse for stalling.

Abdullah stares at Roberta for a moment suspiciously. "It is in the suitcase. If it is not, Sheik Kassem will buy you all the make-up you should want," says Abdullah laughing. Then he stops laughing abruptly and turns to the driver. "Kariff, drive to the airport quickly," Abdullah commands in Arabic.

Kariff nods his head and the car moves forward toward the front gates. When the Rolls Royce gets within three feet of the big doors they start to open slowly. Kariff waits until the gates are fully extended, then he drives the big car through the gates onto the road outside. As he moves away the massive gates close immediately.

The big white car moves quickly down a three lane road. Its headlights piercing the dark night brightening the path ahead. As the car moves further away from Sheik Seid's Palace, the lights in the structure fade away in the distance.

The Sheik's speeding Limo has come to a fork in the road. The lights from the vehicle pick up a sign in Arabic and English. It reads, HARUT CITY AIRPORT 20 kilometers. The big white car moves on to that road. And when it does Kariff presses down on the gas peddle and brings the speedometer up to 90 miles an hour. The white Rolls Royce moves like a flash down the road.

Roberta looks through the car's window into the black night. She is very despondent, because she knows that she is moving closer and closer to her doomed future.

Abdullah's eyes focused through the car's windshield to the road ahead. Kariff eases up on the gas peddle. Abdullah, concerned, becomes aware of the Rolls slowing down its speed and he is puzzled and concerned. "Kariff, why are you slowing down?" asks Abdullah.

"Because, we will not be going to the airport you asshole," declares the chauffeur who is pointing a shiny pearl handle chromium forty-four Magnum in Abdullah's face. The big bodyguard is shocked and Roberta is stunned.

Kariff heads for the shoulder of the road and brings the car to a halt. The driver then pulls off the head cloth covering from his head revealing his true identity. It is Jasmine.

Abdullah's jaw drops open and Roberta screams with shock, joy and relief.

"Jasmine, I knew you'd show up. Thank God," says Roberta

"It was not easy," replies Jasmine while she keeps the gun trained on the big man. "I had to find some padding and dark makeup. Then used,

Kariff's head cloth to smell like him," says Jasmine holding her nose. Roberta laughs to break the tension.

"Abdullah, get your ass out of the car," commands Jasmine. Abdullah screams in anger. He raises his arm to strike Jasmine.

But before he can hit his target the gutsy Jasmine, moves quickly out of harms way. With both hands she pulls the trigger of the big gun. The bullet grazes Abdullah's hand and he screams in pain grabbing his hand to stop the hurt and bleeding. He begins to moan and mumbles in Arabic words of self-pity.

Jasmine throws him the head cloth and the wounded man wraps his bleeding hand. "Alright, now get the hell out of this car before I." screams the angry Jasmine pushing the gun into Abdullah's chest.

The big bodyguard is so frightened and shocked that he stops crying immediately. "Please Jasmine, do not kill me. I will leave. I will leave," says Abdullah as he opens the car door quickly and starts to back out carefully. "May Allah watch over you and guide your path to freedom and," Abdullah forces a thin smile on his lips. "Yes, yes, out," Jasmine impatiently waves the big gun in his face. Abdullah jumps out of the car on to the road. Jasmine shuts the door, and locks it. She pulls off the Goatee from her chin with a throaty 'ouch' and foots the gas pedal down to the floor board.

Abdullah watches the big cars tires spin in place, as they churn and spray sand into his face. After brushing the sand from his eyes he watches in futile indignation as the car speeds down the highway with the fleeing pair. "May Allah curse you both for as long as you live," screams the angry Abdullah. He stands there for a moment and he watches the rear lights of the Rolls Royce fade into the darkness of the road. He adjusts his bandaged hand and starts up the dark highway towards the Palace.

Chapter Twelve
Free At Last

Sheik Seid's white Rolls Royce speeds down the desert high-way heading for Harut City. The glistening headlights light the way for hope and freedom for its occupants.

Roberta is now seated in the front passenger seat alongside of Jasmine. Her head is pressed against the seat, resting. Her face has a look of happy calm relief.

Jasmine drives the big car with ease. She drives with a determined look on her face with her beautiful eyes focused on the dark road ahead of her. After several long moments Jasmine shifts her glance to Roberta and her serious looking expression, dissolves into a smile. "We will be safe soon Roberta," reassures Jasmine.

"Thank God. I had lost all hope," says the tired, but happy Roberta now sitting upright in her seat. She stares at her rescuer for a moment. "Jasmine, I couldn't believe it was you. How did you do it?" asks Roberta.

"It was not easy. Poor Kariff, he will wake up with a lump on the top his head and some hair missing," says Jasmine with pity.

"Jasmine, you are really something. I knew you were a gutsy broad," says Roberta with a little giggle.

"It was just a matter of survival. That is what you must do to live and think as a woman. You will have a big advantage over both men and women because you know how a man thinks. You could use what you know about women as a woman," says Jasmine. with seriousness.

"No, I'm going to Paris to see that doctor who made me what I am. I'm going to make him turn me back to what I used to be," Roberta says with a passion.

"Maybe, he cannot do that. I do not know, let us hope he can," the young intelligent girl supports Roberta.

"Yes, I hope," Roberta says now leaning back in her seat, reflecting Jasmine's comment.

A down hill slope in the roadway reveals the lights of Harut City's outskirts. The Sheik's Rolls Royce comes up a small rise in the highway. It starts down the hill towards the city.

Roberta and Jasmine view the lights of Harut City through the windshield of the big car.

"Harut City is ahead Roberta. We are free," Jasmine's overjoyed voice cries out.

"Yes. I can't wait," says Roberta with anxiety.

"Look, you will not have to worry about getting back to America. I will take you to the American Embassy. You will tell them your story," Jasmine says in confidence.

"No, I can't do that. The news media will pick it up. I'd be a freak in my country and all around the world. I don't want anyone to know what happened to me. Not unless I can be changed back to Robert Anthony. If not, I'll start a new life, or," Roberta pauses.

"There is no or, I understand how you must feel and I can and I will help you," Jasmine says with sympathy and hope.

"You can?" says Roberta.

"Yes, but on one condition," replies Jasmine.

"And what's that?" says Roberta suspiciously.

"That you take me to Paris and America. The Sheik will try to find me. It would not be safe for me here. In the United States I could use my degree to work," explains Jasmine.

"That makes sense. Yes, but you're talking like we already have the passports, your green card and traveling money," says Roberta with realization.

"Do not worry about those things. I have a cousin, who has connections," says Jasmine with confidence.

"Oh, the Arab mafia," says Roberta with humor.

"No, the Mother Superior. She is with the only Catholic church in Harut City," says Jasmine with the same confidence.

"A Mother Superior? She will help?" says Roberta a little puzzled.

"Yes, especially when she finds out what the Sheik has done to you," Jasmine is knowing.

"It sounds too good to be true. A Catholic nun? Do you know who she is?" says Roberta hopefully.

"Yes, from my mother's cousin Peter who became a Catholic when I was going to be sold to the Sheik."

"Peter?" Roberta is puzzled, cutting Jasmine's story off.

"Yes, he changed his name from Ishmael to Peter when he turned Catholic. Anyway, Peter told the Mother Superior about me. So, she went to my father and told him not to sell me to the Sheik. She offered him money but he refused. She could have offered him a million dollars. Still he would have refused," says Jasmine with a sigh of regret. "You see Roberta my father is a die-hard Moslem, he hates Christians, especially my cousin." Jasmine's eyes started to cloud with moisture.

Roberta touches her an comments, "You poor kid. But Jasmine, you've been the Sheik's chattel for almost eight years. A long time has passed. Do you think the Mother Superior is still around?"

"Is the Pope?" Jasmine says smiling.

Roberta thinks for a moment, then smiles hopefully.

"Well, do we have a deal?" Jasmine asks.

"You bet. Let's go talk to the Mother Superior," Roberta's voice is filled with anticipation.

The Sheik's Roll Royce picks up more speed, moves down the hill road and makes its way to Harut City to see the Mother Superior.

The full moon can be seen from the north side of the undraped windows in Sheik Seid's Palace study. The lights in the room are dim and the rays of the big moon falls on Abdullah who is seated in a chair facing the large window. Doctor Kalila is applying a bandage to the big bodyguard's wounded hand.

The Sheik is in his robe talking, and pacing the room as he speaks into the mouth piece of his cellular phone. "Yes. Yes. No. No please do not disturb him. Just tell the Sheik that I regret the big inconvenience I have caused him and that I will make it up to him. Yes, yes. I will call him in the morning and explain in full detail," Sheik Seid completes his a apologetic telephone call. He moves to his desk and places the phone on it. Then he turns to Abdullah and with anger glaring at the man.

"My Sheik, I am so sorry that they have escaped," begs Abdullah in a frightened tone of voice.

"That is alright Abdullah, I do not blame you. How were you to know that Kariff was really Jasmine in disguise," says the most unhappy Sheik calmly. "But," starts Abdullah as the Sheik screams "You should have checked to make sure that it really was Kariff. Was Was that to much for you to do," says the angry wild and stormy Sheik.

THE FIRST LADY

"Please forgive me my Sheik. You are right. I should have checked to see if it was Kariff. Please, please forgive me," pleads Abdullah. "I will go after them, my Sheik. I know that I can find them. Please let me!" Abdullah begs urgently.

"No," answers the Sheik.

Abdullah is shocked and surprised by the Sheik's reply.

The Sheik turns away from his bodyguard to doctor Kalila who had just finished bandaging Abdullah and is giving him an antibiotic shot.

"Jasmine will hide the American. She will help her get out of the country and I do not think that Roberta will go to the American Embassy. I do not think she wants her countrymen, or anyone else to know. Anthony still thinks as a man and he has a lot of pride," says the Sheik with assurance.

"But Ali, what if she does go to the American Embassy?" says doctor Kalila concerned.

Seid smiles broadly. "I am not worried Rashid. Ambassador Kelley is my friend. He is on my payroll. He will turn Roberta over to me immediately and I would give him a big reward," says the Sheik confidently.

"Of course," says doctor Kalila happily.

The Sheik continues, "But, if the Ambassador refuses to turn over his compatriot, which I do doubt. Anthony will have to live in this world as a woman. This will destroy her. But just in case I will have the airport watched. If she is found, I would rather she lives as one of Sheik Kassem's wives," the Sheik laughs masochistically. He is accompanied by the doctor and Abdullah who has joined in this big wish for Roberta's future life.

"Ali, what if you can not find her? What about your gift to Sheik Kassem?" doctor Kalila asks with great concern.

"I will send him a another one, Rashid," says the Sheik simply. His eyes fall on his big bodyguard. "Abdullah,"

Doctor Kalila smiles approvingly. Abdullah understands what his Sheik has just said.

"You know Rashid, I have but one regret," says the Sheik sadly.

"And what is that?" asks the doctor wondering.

"That I will never see my Clint Eastwood gun again," he replies pouting like a spoiled child.

Kalila and Abdullah give their Sheik a sympathetic and sorrowful look.

Chapter Thirteen
A Mother's Help

Jasmine and Roberta have abandoned the Sheik's white Rolls Royce on a dark side street in Harut City. A Saturn sedan moves down the side street, its headlights pick up the Rolls Royce. It stops alongside of the big white car. The passenger door of the Saturn opens and a young Arab man gets out of the passenger seat. He moves quickly to the door of the Sheik's car. The Saturn drives off. The young man opens the car door, gets into the drivers seat and after a few moments, the engine turns over. The big car races away, when it reaches the end of the avenue, it turns the corner and disappears.

The building is the only Catholic church in Harut City and not very large. Its spire is tall, making the Cross on the steeple visible since it's far above all the other house. The property is surrounded by a high, wrought iron picket fence, with a gate at its front entrance.

On the inside grounds there is a path that separates the Church and Rectory. One side of the building houses a Priest and the Monseigenur. On the other side of it lives the nuns with the Mother Superior.

The furnishings in the Church rectory waiting room are very simple. Religious articles decorate the walls. Seated behind a desk is a nun in her late forties wearing a modern day habit that is befitting to Bokuf's climate. She's quite plump, wears no make-up, but she is a good-looking woman. Roberta is sitting in a chair, her legs crossed. She is opposite the desk near the Head Mother's office door. Jasmine is seated on a sofa, next to her cousin, Peter Sabah, a slender, nice looking Arab man in his late thirties.

"Cousin Peter, I hope your friends got rid of the Sheik's car," says Jasmine concerned.

"Jasmine, have no fear, it has been repainted from white to black and by now on its way to Arabia to be sold. The money of the sale to be donated to this Church," Peter says with a happy smile.

"Oh, Peter, you are a savior and a true Catholic," says Jasmine.

"I try to be cousin," Peter says as he smiles with pride.

Roberta has become apprehensive and is very fidgety. She gets up from the chair, sits down next to Jasmine and whispers in her ear. Then Jasmine in a low voice whispers.

"Peter, are you sure you told the Mother Superior everything."

"Yes. Everything. Do not worry my cousin. When she called me this morning, she told me to bring the passport pictures that you both had taken yesterday," Peter whispers.

"Then, it is all set?" Jasmine whispers back.

"I do not know," Peter replies in still unsure whispers.

"But cousin, the Mother Superior told us to bring our passport pictures," whispers Jasmine impatiently.

"She did not say anything else," Peter's whispering continues.

Jasmine moans softly. She turns to Roberta and whispers in her ear. Roberta sighs, uncrosses her legs, puts both feet on the floor and sits like a man.

A man in Arab dress whose face is hidden by his draping cloth head covering comes into the room. Everyone in the room looks at the man with curiosity. All except the nun who nods her head to him and smiles. The man approaches her.

THE FIRST LADY

The sister picks up the phone and presses an intercom button. "He is here, Reverend Mother," says the nun in English. She hangs up the phone, nods her head to the man and he enters the Mother Superior's office. The nun gives the trio a big smile. All three smiled back at the sister, nervously.

The sound of the intercom buzzer is heard once more. The sister picks up the receiver, "Yes, Reverend Mother, yes." The sister hangs up the phone, "The Mother Superior, will see you now," she tells them with a smile.

Roberta and Jasmine follow Peter into the Head Mother's office, all with nervous anticipations.

There is a large crucifix hanging on the wall between the two stained glass windows in the Mother Superior's office. In the corner of the room is a statue of the Virgin Mary that is on a pedestal.

The Mother Superior has a suntanned wrinkled faced, slight of build, probably in her seventies. She is seated in a chair behind an executive desk. Also seated on the left side of her desk is the mystery man. He has taken off his head covering. He is a man in his forties, dark faced, lean, with a jagged red scar across his forehead.

Roberta, Jasmine and Peter, stand before the Reverend Mother, but their eyes are focused on the ominous looking man instead of her. The Mother notices this so she clears her throat and gives the trio a big smile.

Peter recovers quickly. He introduces his charge. "Reverend Mother, this is Roberta Anthony and my cousin Jasmine," Peter smiles nervously.

"Ah, yes, please be seated," says the Reverend Mother with a French accent.

Roberta, Jasmine and Peter sit in chairs that are facing the Mother Superior.

"Jasmine, you were just a little girl when I saw you last. You have grown up and are very beautiful," the Mother says smilingly.

"Oh thank you, Reverend Mother," Jasmine brightens and smiles in reply.

"I heard that your mother left your father right after you were sold to Sheik Seid," the concerned nun relates.

"Yes. I just found out. My mother seems so much happier now," confesses Jasmine.

"That is good to hear. Peter told me what you have gone through and also about all the terrible things that the Sheik has done to you Roberta and the church is going to help you both. This is Hakim," says the Reverend Mother with encouragement.

Roberta, Jasmine, and Peter smile, greeting Hakim with a nod of their heads. Hakim returns the smile with a deadpanned face.

"I told Hakim to help me with the things you will need to get out of Bokuf," she turns to Hakim. "Hakim?" requests the Reverend Mother.

The mystery man digs into his robe and he reveals a long sharp dagger. He pulls out a canvas bag, opens it, then takes out several flat booklets and he places them on the desk. "These are your passports, green card and travel visa's," declares Hakim with a heavy French accent then continues, "One is American and the other is Kuwait, I will need your pictures."

Peter takes an envelope out of his breast pocket, opens it carefully and takes out several passport sized pictures. He then spreads them out on the desk. "Do these look alright, Hakim?" Peter asks.

Hakim quickly studies the pictures, then stares at Roberta and Jasmine for a moment. "They look perfect," replies Hakim. "Now, I will need the names, birth date, places you were born and what address you would like to have on your papers," Hakim says this simply, just the same way he has said to hundreds of people fleeing the country.

Roberta thinking quickly replies. "Ala, ah, Roberta, ah, Mann. August 1st 1974, in California."

THE FIRST LADY

Jasmine frowns as it dawns on her what Roberta said. She starts to laugh, but stops quickly, as Peter, the Mother Superior and Hakim give her a puzzled look.

Roberta has to suppress a giggle and turns her head away from the others. She knows why Jasmine has laughed because of the name of Mann she gave Hakim to use on her passport. It was an ironic slip of the tongue, a joke and only Jasmine got it. With a smile, she turns to Jasmine and winks at her.

"I am sorry, it is just a private joke," says Jasmine to everyone.

Hakim turns to Roberta, "And Miss Mann, what will your address be?" asks Hakim.

"6126 Ensign Ave, North Hollywood, California 91231," Roberta tells Hakim. Hakim writes the information down on a sheet of paper. "Good! now all I would need from you Jasmine, is the name you will use and birth date. I have the rest covered," says Hakim.

Jasmine thinks for a moment. She eyes the stature of the Virgin Mary. "Mary, Mary, Sabah," says Jasmine smiling as she looks at her cousin Peter who is touched by her for honoring his name. "Birth date, October 13, 1980," says Jasmine.

Hakim jots down Jasmine's information. Then like a robot he takes the pictures and pastes them on the proper page of Roberta's and Jasmine's respective passports. He writes down the rest of the information in the required places in each of the passports and travel papers.

Then from his canvas bag he takes out a seal and makes an impression. It is the mark of the seal on passports and papers to make them official. He hands Roberta and Jasmine their traveling I.D's, packs his canvas bag, puts on his head covering and moves to the door. "Good luck to both of you and Bon Voyage," says Hakim. "And Reverend Mother, I will be in touch with you."

"Thank you Hakim," waves the Mother Superior to Hakim.

"Yes, thank you Hakim. We'll never forget what," Roberta doesn't quite finish thanking Hakim as the mystery man is already out the door and gone. "Hum, he must be very busy," Roberta humors. The old nun laughs broadly.

"Reverend Mother, you must have paid him an awful lot of money for our papers," Roberta queries.

"He made a donation to the church. Mr. Hakim is a good catholic," says the Mother proudly.

Roberta and Jasmine are impressed by the nun's explanation of this ominous looking benefactor who they now discover has a heart full of religious charity.

The Mother Superior opens her desk drawer, takes out a manila envelope and holds it out to Roberta. "It is money for your plane fares to Paris, travel expenses and clothes you will need for your trip. I am sorry that there is not enough money for tickets to take you back to America," says the Reverend Mother apologizing, "You have been most generous Mother. I know it's a lot of money for your church to give us," says Roberta in a thankful tone.

"Roberta, do not be concerned about the money. Years ago the church set up a fund. It gets its financing from wealthy donors. We are here to help the many," explains the Mother.

Roberta takes the envelope. "Thank you Mother. Some day I will pay the church back and even much more," vows Roberta.

"And so will I, Reverend Mother," concurs Jasmine. "That is all fine, but at the moment you both have to get out of this country and start new lives," the nun interrupts with concern and encouragement.

"And Mother, do not worry, we will get to America. We will find a way," Roberta responds with new courage and strength.

"God will help both of you," the old nun says knowing in her heart that the Lord will take care of them.

Roberta, Jasmine and Peter smile to the Reverend Mother. They move to the door, Roberta and Jasmine are about to go out of the room

THE FIRST LADY

when Peter turns to the Mother. "Reverend Mother, God shall always bless you and give you a long life," says Peter with a comforting smile.

The old sister gives Peter a 'Thank You' smile and a nod of her head. "Roberta if you cannot make it out there, consider the order of the Nuns," suggests the Mother Superior who was most concerned about Roberta's future new life.

Roberta does not know how to respond to the Mother's suggestion. She bites her lips, forces a big smile and is out the door as Jasmine and her cousin Peter follow her.

When the Reverend Mother is alone, she leans back in her chair. She thinks for a moment, then opens the bottom drawer of her desk and takes out a bottle of French Brandy and a glass. She opens the bottle and pours the Brandy into the glass. She leans back in her chair again, takes a sip of the Brandy and savors the flavor. She then closes her tired eyes. After a moment her lips begin to move, and she whispers, "Paris! My Paris," she smiles.

Helena Laval was remembering her younger days in Paris where she was born and where she grew up. It was the thirties, the depression years. People didn't have much to eat and worse, there was a war in the wind. Her mother took care of her and her three brothers and sister. She washed other peoples clothes to make a few francs a week to help pay some of the bills. Helene Laval remembered how very happy she was when she was growing up. Even with all those terrible things happening then.

The Reverend Mother laughed. She remembered the times that her father came home with a large shopping bag full of food, delicacies, steaks, pheasant, quail, seafood, a rich dessert and a bottle of wine. The food was good and very tasty, the wine superb. It all came from a fine Parisian restaurant where her father worked as a waiter. The owners liked him very much and they knew that he had a big family so they gave him the unfinished dinners left by their rich customers.

A look of pain comes over the Reverend Mother's face and tears fill her eyes. She is remembering the day the German Army invaded France and occupied her Paris and the day that her father and his friends were shot and killed by a German patrol for screaming, "Long Live France." She remembers how her mother grieved and died soon after.

That's when she and her brother's joined the underground and with a vengeance blew up German installations and killed many German soldiers. She was just fourteen years old then.

When the war was over she couldn't live a normal life, the war had changed her. She gave herself to God, became a nun and her mind had been at peace ever since.

The Mother Superior wipes the tears from her eyes. She raises her glass of Brandy and makes a silent toast. To all the people she had loved and then lost.

She downs all of the Brandy and whispers, "Viva La France." She then swings her chair around to the wall and looks up to the Crucifix. She closes her eyes and a happy, reverent smile comes to her lips, she bows her head and begins to pray.

Chapter Fourteen
In The Nick Of Time

A few small private propeller driven planes, two Lear jets, fire and ambulance trucks are parked near the two hangers that are on the southeast side of Harut City's Airport runway. Above the modern passenger terminal building is the Control Tower. The airports lights are lit in all the proper places of the field, terminal and tower. A gated high wired fence is around the property to discourage intruders.

A passenger jet in the sky is coming in for a landing. It sets down on the tarmac perfectly. The name that is written on its fuselage in both 'Arabic and English,' is "Arab Emirate Airlines." The jet moves to a passenger unloading area by the terminal, it comes to a stop and cuts off its engines. A stairway is moved to the passenger door of the jet and locked in place. The door opens and a female Stewardess steps out onto the stairway landing. Then the passengers, a man and woman start unloading, followed by a woman carrying a baby. Behind them a young couple exits holding a child by the hand. Other passengers start unloading and they quickly move past the Stewardess, walk down the steps and head for the terminal. A fuel truck rolls up to the jet and starts to refuel it while the ground crew begins checking over the plane as two Arab baggage men start to unload the luggage from the jet.

An arriving Lear jet taxies to a parking spot not too far from the Emirate jet and plane hanger. Across the plane's fuselage, written in Arabic and English are the words, "Sheik Kassem's Air Camel."

WILLIAM HELLINGER

The Arab Emirate Airlines and Greek Air are the only two Airline ticket desks in the small air terminal. They are serviced by two ticket agents. Arab and European men, women and children, are seated on chairs and benches in the waiting area. Pedestrian traffic moves in and out of the terminal. An Arab immigration man and a customs man in uniform are at their posts as passengers from the Emirate flight come into the terminal.

Several go to the customs man, others report to the immigra- tion counter. Abdullah, with a bandage on his wounded hand appears. He has come into the terminal carrying a suitcase. He is dressed very nicely for his trip to Sheik Kassem's Palace. He is accompanied by one of Sheik Seid's young muscle men. The two men move toward the door leading to the airfield. Karim is with Acmen and Tufa two of the Sheik's other men. The three men nod their heads in recognition to Abdullah's guard. Karim catches Abdullah's depressed look. He stares at the man with pity, then he turns away.

A late model Mercedes taxi pulls up to the curb of the Passenger Air Terminal. The door of the vehicle opens and Jasmine's cousin Peter comes out. He is quickly followed by Roberta and Jasmine who he helps exit from the car. Both of them looked beautiful and well dressed in smart traveling clothes. Each of them carries a suit case. These three move to the entrance of the air depot and enter the building. Then Jasmine and Peter come into the terminal and move to the Arab Emirate Airlines ticket counter.

The Sheik's men Acmen and Tufa are looking in every area of the terminal. Acmen's searching eyes stop suddenly as he sees Roberta. He quickly nudges Karim and points to the two women.

Karim looks in that direction and sees Roberta, Jasmine and Peter at the counter of the airline desk standing behind a very well dressed Arab man. He is being served by a pretty young Arab woman ticket agent. Karim whispers to his man. "Acmen, get the car ready." Acmen moves off quickly.

The female ticket agent hands the Arab man his ticket and says to him "Thank you sir. Your flight leaves in twenty minutes from Gate #2." The man, 'thanks' the agent with a broad smile, and moves away from the counter.

THE FIRST LADY

Peter steps up to the desk. "Two one way tickets to Paris, please," Peter requests.

The young ticket agent smiles as she looks at her computer and checks for seats that are available on that flight. "Yes, we have two seats in row C. One is a window seat. Would that be alright sir?" says the agent.

Peter looks over to Jasmine, who indicates a 'yes' to him with a broad smile. He turns back to the agent. "That will be fine," says Peter digging into the pocket of his jacket.

"That is flight 69, gate #1. It leaves in forty minutes. The names please," asks the woman.

A sullen Abdullah with his guard moves to Sheik Kassem's Lear jet. A large bearded Arab man dressed in flight clothes stands by the entrance of the plane. When they reach the jet, Abdullah sees through the windshield of the jet's cockpit an Arab pilot in uniform seated behind the controls of the plane reading an 'Arab Penthouse' magazine.

Karim observes Roberta, Jasmine and Peter as they move away from the ticket counter and go towards the customs desk. He stands behind an elderly Asian man and woman who are at that moment are being taken care of by the customs man.

Peter hands Jasmine the airline tickets. "Well cousin, I hope everything goes well for you and Roberta, if I ever see you again, I hope to see Robert," says Peter smiling.

Roberta gives Peter a smile of hope and a "thank you."

Jasmine with moist eyes hugs him. "My dear cousin, I love you and thank you for all your help. I will be in touch with you, no matter what."

Peter holds back his tears as he hugs Jasmine.

Then Roberta and Jasmine move off with quick long steps toward the terminal exit.

Karim watches Peter leave the terminal and then turns back to his surveillance of Roberta and Jasmine.

The customs man completes his inspection of the elderly couple's baggage and they move off toward the passenger loading area of Gate #1.

Roberta and Jasmine step up to the counter, put their suitcases on the counter and open them. The custom man carefully examines their belongings while eyeing the two women suspiciously. He completes his inspection, closes their bags and gives them back. "Your passports," he declares in a very heavy English Arab accent.

Roberta gives her passports to the man. He stares at her for a moment. He opens Roberta's passport and with the turn of each page he looks up at Roberta with suspicion. When he gets to Roberta's picture his eyes move from the photo to Roberta. He repeats this action several times. Roberta holds her breath. Satisfied, the customs man completes his inspection of Roberta's passport and returns it to her. Roberta breathes a sigh of relief.

The customs man gives Roberta a big smile. "Thank you and have a good trip," he says. Under his breath in a very sexy tone of voice "You are so, very beautiful."

Roberta plays along with his remark as she smiles broadly, winking at him. With passport in hand and her suitcase and a very sexy movement of her hips, Roberta goes off toward Gate #1.

The customs man's eyes follow Roberta's rear end until she disappears through the door. With a big smile on his face he displays great approval. He then goes to the next customer. It is Jasmine.

Jasmine is biting her lips to keep from laughing. As she hands the titillated man her passport she flirts with him and gives him a sexy smile.

The customs man with a twinkle in his eye grins sensually at Jasmine. He is so distracted by Jasmine's flirtation, that he makes a very quick once over of her papers. He stares at Jasmine longingly.

Jasmine gives the man a big, 'thank you smile' and says very sweetly in Arabic. "May I have my papers, please."

"Oh, yes, of course," says the customs man soberly in Arabic. He gives Jasmine back her passport, but before the man could say another word, Jasmine moves quickly away toward Gate #1 where the passenger are boarding. Karim and Tufa follow Jasmine.

A black limousine approaches slowly down the back road and pulls up to the gates and stops. A man emerges from the drivers seat. He leaves the motor and the car's headlights on and approach- es the locked gates. The light from the car's headlights hit the man, revealing, Acmen. He is carrying a large wire cutter. He fixes the cutter to the gates chained padlock and in one snap the lock and chain is cut in two. Quickly, Acmen swings open the gates and then he gets back into the car and drives through the gates and stops when he clears them. Acmen gets out of the car, shuts the gates, then gets back into the limo. The car rolls toward an airport hanger.

Chapter Fifteen
The Assault

At Gate #1 loading area the passenger baggage is being placed on board the Arab Emirate Airline Jet. Roberta, Jasmine and other passengers are waiting to board the plane

Karim and Tufa are standing nearby in the shadows of the area.

Karim leans over to Acmen and whispers something in his ear.

Acmen nods his head and moves off and disappears. Karim starts to move toward Roberta and Jasmine. Suddenly Jasmine's cousin Peter comes in through Gate #1's door and runs to Roberta and Jasmine. Karim stops for a moment.

"Cousin Peter," says Jasmine surprised.

"I had to come back to see you take off. I don't know if I will ever see you again," says Peter lovingly.

"Do not worry cousin, you will see me again and soon," says Jasmine smiling.

Acmen's limo travels around the back of the hanger and heads toward the Arab Emirate jet.

Abdullah and his guard are standing by the door of Kassem's Air Camel watching the fuel truck refueling the jet. From the corner of

Abdullah's eyes he catches the black limousine moving very slowly toward the plane. When the limousine goes past the jet he sees Acmen behind the wheel. Abdullah now observes the black limo riding in the direction of the Arab Emirate jet. It stops not too far from the planes tarmac. A few moments later he sees a man approach the car, who says something to the driver. The man taps the door with his hand and quickly moves off. The limo is in motion again. It shifts closer to the Emirate jets tarmac. The look on Abdullah's face reveals, that he knows what is going to happen.

Karim sees Jasmine and Peter in conversation and he moves in very slowly toward the trio. He gets behind Roberta. Jasmine and her cousin Peter are distracted, from not noticing Karim. Karim sees Tufa come in and when he reaches him, Tufa waves his hand indicating that everything is set.

Karim reaches into his jacket pocket and pulls out a pistol. Tufa follows suit. In unison the two men move in very close to Roberta and Jasmine. Karim moves alongside of Jasmine while Tufa gets in close to Roberta's back. Karim shoves his gun into Jasmine's side as at the same time Tufa pushes his gun into Roberta's back. When Roberta and Jasmine feel the barrel of a gun pressed against them, they are stunned. Both women turn to their assailants, when they see that it is Karim and another man they are surprised. At that moment Peter gets blinded by a little Arab girl who is waving her big stuffed teddy bear into his face. Peter is unaware of what is happening to Roberta and Jasmine.

Karim leans into Jasmine's ear. "Jasmine, do not say a word. You and Roberta will come with us. If you refuse, we will have to shoot you both," declares Karim in Arabic quietly and very firmly.

"Karim please let us go, please," pleads Jasmine in Arabic quietly.

"I am sorry Jasmine I must do this, if not the Sheik will have me killed," says Karim apologetically in a whisper.

"Yes," Jasmine agrees. She then leans into Roberta.

"Roberta, we must go with them or else," warns Jasmine warningly with a phony smile on her face.

THE FIRST LADY

Roberta turns to Karim with a big smile and then whispers to Jasmine. "Can't we talk this big jerk out of it?" asks Roberta giving Karim another big smile.

"I am afraid not," says Jasmine again smiling with tight lips.

"Shit. We've got to do something," suggests Roberta with a forced smile.

"We must go now," orders Karim to Jasmine very quietly in Arabic.

"Yes, but please let me make some kind of an excuse to my cousin before we go with you," whispers Jasmine pleading in Arabic.

"Alright, but make it quick," whispers Karim impatiently. Jasmine thinks for a moment, then turns to Peter who is still unaware of their plight.

"Peter, ah, Roberta must go to the ladies room urgently. I will go with her," says Jasmine calmly holding out the plane tickets to Peter. "Check us in."

"But cousin, it is almost time to get aboard. Roberta can you not hold it until then?" says Peter.

"Peter, when a lady has to go, she has to go," says Roberta with a nervous laugh.

"Alright, but hurry," says Peter taking the tickets from Jasmine.

"Passengers for flight 69 to Paris, the plane will leave in eighteen minutes. Boarding now," says the air Terminal announcer in Arabic. "Passengers for flight 69 to Paris leaves in eighteen minutes. You may board the plane now," says the air terminal announcer now in English.

"Don't worry Peter we'll be back in time," says Roberta giving Peter a big smile.

Jasmine nudges Peter to get on the plane. Peter smiles back and follows the other passengers who are starting to board the jet.

Karim waits until Peter is caught up in the crowd. "Let us go now," commands Karim. With guns still trained on Roberta and Jasmine, Karim and Tufa head for the other side of the tarmac.

The black limousine's lights are off. But the lights from the airport reflect on its steel body. A shadowy light that comes through the cars windshield hits Acmen's face who is seated behind the wheel of the limo. His eyes are focused in the direction of the Emirate jet. He sees Karim and Tufa with their two prisoners come around the Emerate jets tarmac towards him. Acmen's face lights up with a joyful smile.

At that same time, Abdullah sees Karim and Tufa, moving very quickly and silently towards the black limousine with Roberta and Jasmine.

Jasmine feels that she and Roberta are trapped and there is nothing they could say to Karim and Tufa to get them to set them free. She turns to Roberta. "Roberta, we were so close too getting away. We are now doomed," says Jasmine hopelessly.

"Oh yeah, not on your life and mine," says Roberta who comes to a quick decision. She turns to Karim. Stares at him for a moment, then comes to a complete halt jarring the big man. Tufa and Jasmine are taken by surprise and they are both forced to stop.

"Keep moving," Karim demands in Arabic shoving the barrel of the gun into Roberta's ribs.

"Jasmine, tell this big jerk that I'm not going anywhere until he hears me out," says Roberta with her life on the line.

Jasmine figures that Roberta is making a desperate move for their release or escape. "Karim, Roberta wants to tell you something," says Jasmine in Arabic.

"No. You tell her to move, or else," orders Karim now very angry.

"Roberta, he is very mad, he wants you to keep moving or else," warns Jasmine with concern.

"Yeah, well you tell that bastard that he can hear what I have to say or he can kill me right here and now." says Roberta who is even angrier.

Jasmine is shocked at Roberta's request. "Are you sure that you want me to tell him that?"

"Absolutely," says Roberta.

"I do not think it is a very good idea," says Jasmine now very worried about Roberta's life.

"You bet your ass I do. I got nothing to lose or live for," says Roberta with a tone of finality in her voice.

Jasmine knows that Roberta meant what she said, so she gets closer to Karim. "Karim, Roberta said either you hear what she has to say or you can shoot her right here and now," Jasmine informs Karim softly and firmly.

Karim becomes even angrier. Then after a few moments his mood begins to soften and he motions for Roberta to speak.

Jasmine, breathes a sigh of relief. The strain on her face slowly diminishes.

Roberta understands Karim's response and gives the big man a thank you gesture. Then Roberta looks straight into Karim's eyes and not once do her eyes become detached from his eyes. "Jasmine, tell him, Sheik Seid is a camel turd," says Roberta calmly.

Jasmine is shocked and puzzled by Roberta's comment about the Sheik.

"And tell him what a terrible thing Sheik Seid has done to him. Taking out his eye, slicing up his face, making him look ugly. Tell Karim how much he cared about you and protected you, and that he should not be loyal to this shithead Sheik Seid. He should let us go," says Roberta with a last hope of freedom.

Jasmine takes a deep breath and begins to repeat in Arabic, Roberta's words of condemnation of the Sheik Seid.

Acmen is puzzled when he sees that Karim, Tufa and their prisoners have stopped walking. He is concerned and he starts to get out of the limo. He then stops and thinks that he had better stay in the car and wait to see what happens next. Karimshows no emotion as he listens to Jasmine. "and that you should not be loyal to a shithead like Sheik Seid and that you should let us go free," Jasmine says as she holds her breath knowing that Karim is digesting what she had just told him. Roberta and Jasmine are both waiting with baited breaths for the big man's response.

Tufa is concerned by what Jasmine has just told Karim. He glares at the big man. Karim's answer is the jamming of the barrel of his gun into Roberta's kidney. Jasmine's face became somber. She gasps.

"Karim, does this mean you're not interested?" says Roberta trying to make light of Karim's response to her request.

Karim presses the gun with a little more force into Roberta's side. "Now move." commands Karim in Arabic. Roberta stays in place.

"Roberta, I think we better keep moving," says Jasmine in a hopeless frightened tone of voice.

Tufa lets out a big belly laugh. "Karim she is just another stupid American who thinks that they can talk their way out of anything," Tufa says this in Arabic laughing sardonically.

Karim laughs at Tufa's remark. Then he and Tufa prod their prisoners to start moving toward the black limo. Roberta shrugs her shoulders as she and the despondent Jasmine began to walk towards their impending fates.

Karim touches the patch on his eye as he moves forward in thought. Then he runs his fingers across the ugly scar on his disfigured cheek. A look of hate and contempt comes over his face. Karim's mind flashes a picture of Sheik Seid's face, the face of the man who destroyed his appearance.

THE FIRST LADY

When Acmen sees Karim, Tufa and their prisoners approaching the car, he snaps on the limo's headlights instantly then gets out of the vehicle and greets them. "Sheik Seid will be most happy with their capture. I know he will reward us handsomely," says Acmen with a big smile. Then he opens the back door of the big car quickly. "Get in," says Acmen ominously. Now Roberta and Jasmine do not move "I said get in." orders Acmen forcefully.

"No. I'm not going." screams Roberta in defiance.

"I am not going either," Jasmine joins in.

Acmen and Tufa grab the two women by their arms and start to pull them to the open door of the car, trying to push them into the back seat. Roberta and Jasmine resist the two men.

Karim, with no expression on his face, just stands there looking at the two men struggling with the two prisoners. Karim lets out a big grunt and pans his gun to Acmen and Tufa. "Stop. Let them go." commands Karim stunning the two men with this request.

"Karim., what do you think you are doing?" yells Acmen. "Set them free, now. Release them." orders Karim pushing his gun into the faces of the two men.

Roberta smiles and winks to Jasmine knowingly. She had a feeling that their plea would turn Karim around.

When Acmen and Tufa release Roberta and Jasmine, they push them into Karim's gun, causing Karim to drop his weapon. The two men jump the big man and knock him to the ground. Karim tries to retrieve his gun, but Tufa steps on the big man's groping hand and kicks the gun away. Karim struggles with the two men while trying to get to his feet, but he is unable to.

Roberta and Jasmine try to jump into the fray to help their benefactor, but they can not. The swinging arms, fists, legs and feet, keep the two women away from the battling trio.

Abdullah, who has been observing all the action around the black limousine is shocked when he sees that Karim is in trouble.

The truck refueling Kassem's Air Camel, is starting to move away from the jet. Abdullah sees that his guard is watching the truck as it clears the plane and move up the road. Abdullah hits the distracted guard with a rabbit punch and the man crumbles to the ground unconscious. Before anyone on the Lear jet can react, Abdullah races off into the direction of the black limo.

Abdullah reaches the car and sees that Acmen and Tufa have the struggling Karim pinned to the ground while Roberta and Jasmine are trying to pull the two men off the big man.

Acmen snatches up Karim's gun from the ground nearby and points it to Karim's head. Abdullah quickly jumps onto the two assailants and the force knocks the gun out of Acmen's hand. Roberta, Jasmine and Karim are shocked and surprised to see Abdullah there helping them.

The Sheik's four men fight each other in a life and death combat. Roberta and Jasmine are cheering Karim and Abdullah.

The battle is over quickly, Acmen and Tufa are on the ground unconscious and bloody.

"Abdullah, Karim, I, we want to thank you for saving our lives," says Jasmine in Arabic and hugs both men.

Roberta then makes a victory sign to her two rescuers while smiling gratefully to them.

"Now go quickly, do not miss your flight," says Karim to Jasmine.

"What will you and Abdullah do now?" asks Jasmine.

"We will be alright Jasmine, is that not right Karim?" says Abdullah. Karim smiles to Jasmine and nods his head to her in assurance.

"May Allah bless both of you and watch over you," Jasmine says with great sincerity.

THE FIRST LADY

Roberta and Jasmine smile at the two men and then head for the Arab Emirate jets tarmac with speed.

Karim and Abdullah wait until the women moved around the tarmac to safety. Satisfied they are safe, Karim and Abdullah start for the limousine, they then see Sheik Seid's man and two of Kassem' s men running towards them. Quickly, Karim and Abdullah get into the car with Karim in the drivers seat. He flips the ignition key on and the big car's engine turns over and with his foot pressed heavy on the gas pedal he sets the car in motion. The black vehicle roars off in the direction of the rear gate, just as Kassem's men and Seid's man arrive.

Karim looks into the limo's rear view mirror and sees the three men throw up their hands in disgust and he gives a sigh of relief and laughs.

"Well, we got away from them, Karim, but where do we go from here?" asks Abdullah concerned.

"Abdullah, do not worry. My uncle is a Bedouin. I know where to find his tribe, he will help us." Karim assures him with confidence.

The black limousine reaches the rear gate rapidly. Abdullah gets out of the car and goes to the gate. He is overjoyed to find it unlocked. As he swings it open he hears the sounds of roaring jet engines overhead and looks up to the sky. Karim sticks his head out of the open car window and looks skyward. They both see the Emirate passenger jets lights flashing as it climbs into the dark sky and disappear into a bank of clouds.

"They are both safe, Karim. Thanks to Allah and you." says a happy Abdullah with a big smile as he climbs into the limo. Karim smiles, drives the black car through the open gate and speeds off into the darkness of the desert roadway.

At the Palace the two guards with bruised faces, Tufa and Acmen stand before Sheik Seid with great trepidation. They relate what had happened at the airport. The Sheik curses them, pounds his fists on the desk and screams, "You cowardly, dumb, stupid, snail brained weaklings."

"But my Sheik," says the frightened Tufa. "It was Karim and Abdullah," cries Tufa.

"Yes my Sheik, it was them and we fought with our lives. But they had guns, we could do nothing," says Acmen with desperation in his voice.

"My Sheik, please forgive us. We would have given up our lives to keep them from escaping," says Tufa with bravado.

The Sheik is silent, his face is riddled with anger and hate. Then after a moment, a sadistic smile comes over his face. "You both will go to Paris immediately. Do not return, until you find Roberta and Jasmine and kill them." screams Sheik Seid in a venomous hiss.

Tufa and Acmen breath a sigh of relief. They smile, bow their heads and lay prostrate before their Lord and Master.

Chapter Sixteen
Paris City of Hope

The bright early morning sun comes up to its apex in the sky. The Arab Emirate Passenger Plane comes in through the white clouds. It flies over the city heading for the Charles DeGaulle airport. The Arab passenger plane reaches the busy airport, lands and taxies to a tarmac and parks. The big jet's doors open and all the passengers including Roberta and Jasmine, begin to deplane. Like ants, they file into the modern Charles DeGulle airport building.

Roberta and Jasmine are relieved and happy. They move toward baggage, immigration and customs exits. They join the other passengers who are retrieving their baggage which is shooting down the luggage ramp and on to a carousel. Roberta and Jasmine spot their luggage which they grab and load it on to a baggage cart nearby. They wheel the cart towards the customs entrance. Other passengers from their flight and other flights, head in the same direction.

Roberta and Jasmine reached the customs area and enter the room where Customs officials, three men and two women are searching through passengers luggage very throughly and very quickly. Roberta and Jasmine push their luggage cart to the Custom's line where other people are waiting. When they get on the line they feel a little uneasy.

Roberta and Jasmine hold their breaths playing the demure helpless females. Coyly they smile at the two customs agents who are carefully inspecting their luggage. The agents maintain their serious looks, while examining their passports and Jasmine's green card slowly. The customs

WILLIAM HELLINGER

men complete their examination and then welcome Roberta and Jasmine into their country. The men give them big flirtatious smiles when they leave.

Roberta and Jasmine leave the busy airport terminal into the heavy Paris traffic pushing their baggage cart. They hail a taxi that had just pulled up to the curb. A passenger and a young man get out of the cab.

The young man sees Roberta and Jasmine standing there. He whistles at them and in French says, "You are both beautiful, sexy and magnificent." Roberta does not understand, but Jasmine gives him a big smile. The taxi driver opens the trunk, takes their suitcases and places them into the trunk. Then the cabby moves to the passenger door, swings it open and Roberta and Jasmine get into the cab.

The cabby now in the driver's seat turns to Roberta and Jasmine. "Where to, beautiful ladies?" says the smiling cabby in French.

Roberta gives the driver a blank look, but Jasmine smiles knowingly. "Any inexpensive hotel on the Champs d'Elysee?" asks Jasmine in perfect French.

"Ah, Yes. Yes, madam. I know just the place," replies the cabby in French giving Jasmine a big smile.

The taxi leaves the air terminal, tout de suite and ascends into the Paris morning traffic. As he drives through the city, the cabby looks into his rear view mirror and says, "Ladies, you are now in the city of love, good food and famous landmarks. This includes the Arc De Triumph, the Eiffel Tower and the Nortre Dame Cathedral." Roberta and Jasmine are impressed.

The taxi moves down the Champs d' Elysees and turns off on a side street. The cab continues down the street and stops at the entrance of an old and very well kept four story building. The sign on the marque states that it is 'THE LORRAINE HOTEL'.

The cab driver gets out of the car, opens the passenger door and Roberta and Jasmine emerge. The cabby quickly opens the trunk and takes out the women's luggage. Roberta and Jasmine go up the three steps leading to the Lorraine's entrance. The cabby is close behind them carrying

THE FIRST LADY

their suitcases. The trio go into the building though its old brass and glass revolving doors.

Roberta, Jasmine and the cabby enter the hotel lobby and see that it is not busy. At the Registration desk is the clerk. He is a suave looking man in his sixties keeping busy behind the counter sorting out hotel bills and placing them into the mail boxes of the hotel's guests. Roberta and Jasmine start for the desk. An elderly couple comes out of the elevator and move past them smiling, waving to the desk clerk, who smiles back at them. The happy couple exit out through the hotel's brass and glass revolving doors.

Roberta and Jasmine go to the desk, as the cabby sets their suitcases down and then approaches the desk clerk.

"Maurice. How are you?" asks the cabby in French.

"Ah. Louie, I'm well," replies Maurice the desk clerk in French. "And you?" continues Maurice.

"Real great, I can still go all night," says Louie the cabby. They both began to laugh, including Jasmine.

Roberta as before does not understand what is going on, but this time she gives a little titter.

When the laughter dies down Louis moves up to Maurice and places his arm around the man's shoulder. "Maurice, I want you to take care of these two beautiful ladies. They do not have much money. Give them a good room, but, for as little money as you can, okay?" Louie speaks for this favor.

"But of course," says Maurice. Jasmine smiles broadly.

"Madam's, Maurice, my brother-in-law will take good care of you. Bonjour," Louis now speaks in broken English.

Roberta and Jasmine are surprised by the cabbies English.

"Thank you Louie, thank you," says Roberta smiling with jubilance.

Jasmine takes some bills out of her bag and gives them to Louis. "Louis, I hope this is enough," says Jasmine.

"Beautiful ladies, welcome to Paris. Please, keep the money. Have dinner on Louie Chairamonte," says Louie with love. He shoves the money back into Jasmine's hands, winks at the women and exits out, leaving through the revolving doors of the hotel.

"My brother-in-law Louie has a heart of gold. Ladies, the Lorraine is very old, very clean. I promise that your hotel bill will fit your budget," says Maurice in broken English.

His English surprises Roberta and Jasmine and they give the desk clerk a broad thankful smile.

Their Lorraine hotel room door swings open and Roberta and Jasmine go into the room. Maurice follows them carrying their luggage. Roberta extends a tip to Maurice, he hesitates for a moment, then takes the money and holds it up.

"The bellboy will be in tomorrow. The poor man just buried his ninety-seven year old mother. I will save the tip for him. If you need anything, please call me," explains Maurice.

"Thank you Maurice," says Roberta.

Maurice smiles, gives Roberta the key, leaves the room closing the door behind him.

"For Paris, I cannot believe that this is happening to us," Jasmine says in awe.

"Jasmine we just lucked out. Let's hope the rest of our stay in Paris is just as lucky for us," Roberta warns.

"Roberta, I have a feeling that everything is going to turn out real fine," Jasmine says while pressing a comforting touch to Roberta's arm.

"From your lips to Allah's ears," Roberta prays. Jasmine pulls the drapes away from the windows in the room and the sun comes through the two windows, brightening up the room. "You know this is a nice room," Jasmine approves.

"Yeah. A nice big bed. The furniture fits the old décor." Roberta sits on the bed. "Let's hope the low cost of this room doesn't include sharing the room with bed bugs," says Roberta laughing now with Jasmine joining in.

"You know, for an old joint this bed feels pretty comfortable," Roberta tells Jasmine as she starts bouncing up and down on the bed with her back side.

Roberta and Jasmine place their suitcase on the bed. They both open up their suitcases and takes out their clothes and begin hanging up their clothes in the closet.

Roberta stops for a moment. "Jasmine, I think I'd better find out where Doctor Faux's office is and try to see him today," she says hopefully.

"Maybe he is not in town," Jasmine ventures.

"Well, if not today perhaps tomorrow, or whenever he's available to see me. Hopefully he tells me what I want to hear. Then we can go to the U.S. Embassy and tell them everything," Roberta finalizes.

"Roberta, what if the news is bad", Jasmine tests Roberta.

"Then, I don't know what I will do," Roberta says in a frightening tone of voice.

"Roberta, do not say that. Everything is going to be alright, I know it is. If not, we will think of a way to get out of France," Jasmine encourages.

"How, win the French Lottery, rob a bank?" Roberta adds black humor.

"We can always sell our bodies," replies Jasmine in jest.

"Oh my God, I'll die first," says Roberta with an ironic laugh.

"Alright, Roberta," says Jasmine laughing. "Before you have to do anything drastic let us find Doctor Faux's office and make an appointment with him," Jasmine says with a small giggle as she quickly goes to the night table to search for the Paris phone book, When Jasmine finds it, she sits at the edge of the bed thumbing through the pages. Roberta sits next to her.

"D, e, f, yes. Here it is. Doctor Girard Faux," says Jasmine picking up the phone on the night table and dialing the operator. "Operator, will you please give me 442-246, thank you," Jasmine says in French. Roberta waits with baited breath.

"Yes, may I speak to Doctor Faux please. Oh. Oh I see," says Jasmine in French with a disappointed look on her face. "Yes, I see. Yes. Yes. Oh! Then, will it be possible to see Doctor Mallet today. Yes, it is very important. At 1 P.M. Yes that will be fine. Thank you," Jasmine finishes her telephone conversation, hangs up and pauses before she tells Roberta the news.

"Well?" declares Roberta eagerly.

"Three months ago," says Jasmine with difficulty, she stops, then takes a breath and starts again. "Roberta, Doctor Faux went on a climbing expedition. It was Mount Everest. Then half way up, they were caught in an avalanche. He and his group were never found." Roberta is stunned and speechless.

Jasmine puts her arms around Roberta to console her. "Wait Roberta, it is not all that bad. There is still some hope. It seems that an associate of Doctor Faux, a Doctor Mollet, has taken over his practice. I am sure that he could help you," says Jasmine trying to cheer her up. "And Roberta, I do not think that you should tell Doctor Mallet the reason why Doctor Faux transformed you. He may want to protect Doctor Faux's good name. Be careful," Jasmine warns her. "I agree," says Roberta. "If he asks me why I want to be changed back, I'll just tell him I made a mistake. Being a woman isn't any fun and," Roberta can't continue. She was lost in her thoughts for a moment. "Then, I'll tell him that I still have that male urge to fuck all women that I am aroused by.

"You do?" says Jasmine surprised.

"Jasmine, with all the new hormones they shot into me, I really don't know what my feelings are. So if you, Jasmine had to ask me then, this Doctor, eh, Mallet, will surely believe my request for a recycle," explains Roberta.

"I agree. We are seeing him this afternoon at 1:00. Roberta, I have a feeling that everything is going to work out for you," Jasmine responds. "Jasmine, Robert Anthony will be born again." cries Roberta.

Chapter Seventeen
To Be or Not To Be

The Lafayette Medical Building is a modern structure that overlooks the Seine river. The area is heavy with car traffic while the pedestrian traffic is light for this time of the day. A taxi comes down the street and stops in front of the Medical building. Roberta and Jasmine descend from the cab. They follow other people entering the building. In the lobby several people are waiting for an elevator. Roberta and Jasmine join them. When the elevator stops at the lobby it is empty. But, on its way up it is filled to capacity. There is silence on the elevator. It makes stops at each floor discharging the passengers. When it reaches the tenth floor, Roberta and Jasmine are just getting off. A passenger, an elderly Frenchmen who is standing behind them, pinches both Roberta's and Jasmine's behinds. He is outside the doors of the elevator before Roberta and Jasmine can complain.

"Now I know how a woman feels when she's attacked from the rear," says Roberta giggling.

"This was the first time for me and it was not too bad," Jasmine is laughing out loud.

Their laughter dies down as they reach the hallway where doctor's officers of all the different cosmetic specialties flank the corridor. Each surgeon specialized in different parts of the anatomy, from the lifting of the feet, to the lifting of the scalp.

WILLIAM HELLINGER

When they get to the last office down the hall they see written across double glass doors, Doctor Girard Faux, Surgeon Of Cosmetic and Body Renovation.

Roberta and Jasmine enter the office and immediately they are escorted into Doctor Philip Mollet's private office. Doctor Mollet is a man in his mid-fifties and is seating behind his desk.

The doctor smiles and with a hand gesture, he indicates for Roberta and Jasmine to be seated. As Roberta is getting into the chair, her eye catches a framed photograph hanging on the wall behind the doctor's desk. A black ribbon is draped around its frame. It is a color picture of a nice looking man in his early forties, who has a big smile on his face. At first Roberta is puzzled. Then she assumes that it must be the picture of the man who illegally performed the transsexual surgery that transformed him into a woman.

Thoughts run through Roberta's mind. She has come to Paris to have Doctor Faux reverse her gender back to being Robert the big male stud. But now he is dead, gone forever. It is impossible for the good doctor to do the rebirth. Roberta's lips begin to form words. She is silent, but she wants to shout out loud, scream how she really feels about the man who turned Robert into Roberta. But she was afraid to screw up things with Doctor Mollet who might help her. Instead she screams the words in her mind. "I'm happy that Doctor Girard Faux is dead! Fuck the bastard, he got what he deserved. I hope that God made the good doctor suffer a slow agonizing death when he was buried under tons of snow and ice that rolled over him. And that the dirty fucken, bastard, prick, should burn in hell for the blackest sin that any man could do to another human being."

Doctor Mollet sees that Roberta is staring at Faux's photo on the wall and has her eyes closed as if in reverence. "Isn't that a nice photograph of Doctor Faux?" says Doctor Mollet who speaks English with a delightful French accent.

"Yes, it is," answers Roberta forcing herself to speak. Jasmine looks over at Roberta, surprised. Then she looks at Doctor Faux's picture. "I agree," says Jasmine who wants to scream invectives at Faux's photo.

"It was a recent picture of Girard. He gave it to me the day before he left for his Mt. Everest climb." Mollet's smiling face turns somber.

THE FIRST LADY

"When I was informed of his unfortunate accident, I placed his photograph up there in memory and to mourn him. He was my colleague and my very good friend. Doctor Qirard Faux was a great surgeon. He will be remembered by the medical profession all over the world for his advance techniques in transsexual surgery and Plastic surgery renovations of the body. There will never be another one like him," Doctor Mollet is overcome with a reverence for his friend.

"Thank God," mumbles Roberta.

"What did you say?" inquires Doctor Mollet suspiciously.

"I said, thank God he had friends like you who will miss him and all his advance techniques," again Roberta gives him a forced smile.

"Oh, yes, I will miss him and so will many others," Doctor Mollet says sadly.

"Doctor Mollet, I'll miss him even more. Eight months ago Doctor Faux, performed transsexual surgery on me," Roberta seriously states.

"You are not a real woman," the surprised doctor cuts in.

"Can't you tell?" Roberta says in a surprised tone. "No, you look perfect. What is it that you want from me?" a smiling Mollet inquires.

"I wish to be changed back to what I was, a man," replies Roberta.

"May I ask why?' the puzzled doctor asks.

"I realize that I've made a mistake. I can no longer live as a woman. If I can't be helped, I'll end my life," Roberta's answer is really serious.

"Do not speak that way, I will try to help you. I will give you a complete examination to see if I can help you. That is the least I can do for one of Doctor Faux's patients," as Doctor Mollet responds to Roberta he punches a button on his office intercom. In a moment a female voice in French answers. "Yes Doctor Mollet."

"Marie, please prepare Ms. Anthony for an examination," replies Doctor Mollet in French.

"Yes, doctor," responds Marie in French.

"Ms. Anthony, my nurse will prepare you for your examin-ation. Please go into that room." Mollet points to a door, "She will get you ready for me," says Mollet smiling.

"Doctor, can I go in with her?" asks Jasmine. "I do not see why not," says the doctor.

When Roberta, and Jasmine are about to go into the examination room, Roberta's eyes focus again on Doctor Mollet's memorial to Doctor Faux. Roberta closes her eyes as though she was memorizing Doctor Faux's smiling face in the photo. Then she opens her eyes quickly and moves into the examination room with Jasmine following her.

Nurse Marie gives Roberta a white examination gown. Roberta goes behind a screen to undress and get into the gown. While she is taking off her clothes she keeps thinking of Doctor Faux's smiling face in the photo.

While she lays on the examination table and is being examined by Doctor Mollet, her legs are apart and her feet are in the stirrups. Her mind is manufacturing thoughts, creating pictures. She sees Doctor Faux's cold, wet face climbing with the rest of his party up the shear, snowy and icy covered slopes of Mt. Everest. Then she hears the sudden roaring sound high above the climbers and then sees tons of loosened snow, ice and rock cascading swiftly down the mountain. It is growing as it descends toward the climbers. She sees them panic as they all look up at the avalanche coming down at them. They try to get out of its path. But too late, the mass of white death rolls over them and carries them down the mountain slopes, burying the entire group under a fifty foot blanket of snow, ice and rock.

Roberta was not happy with her visions of the other climbers in Faux's party that lost their lives. She felt pity and sorrow for them. But she was content with Doctor Faux's demise and she wanted to see that. So again she brought her fantastic visions to the place under the snow where Doctor Faux was buried. He was still alive. He hadn't suffocated yet. He was in a air pocket. She sees him trying vainly to claw his way out of the snow above him, to get out of his white tomb. But to no avail, he was too exhausted. It was freezing cold, his body was getting numb he was losing air and it was hard for him to breath. Roberta's mind tried to fathom what Faux's last thoughts could be. Yes, he must have asked God why he had to die this terrible death. God must have answered his question and said, "It was because of what you did to Robert Anthony. Vanity and greed was your ultimate sin." Roberta knew that Doctor Faux couldn't argue that point with the supreme master. So she thought that he must have told God that God was right for punishing him. Then Roberta thought of what Doctor Faux might have sobbed and screamed out with his last breath, "GOD PLEASE FORGIVE ME!"

Doctor Mollet completed his examination. "Ms. Anthony, I am finished, you can dress now," Doctor Mollet exclaims as he takes off his surgical rubber gloves and throws them into the medical disposal basket.

Roberta, raises herself up from the table and sits at the edge of the examination table awaiting for the doctor's verdict with anticipation.

A concerned Jasmine is sitting in a chair near a window where a view of the city could be seen. She gives Roberta an encouraging smile.

Doctor Mollet approaches Roberta. "Ms. Anthony, Doctor Faux made you perfect. Beautiful inside and outside as though you were born with those attributes." Then the doctor's smile, turns to a sympathetic look. "But, unfortunately, I cannot reverse Doctor Faux's procedure," Doctor Mollet says this with finality.

"Why?" asks Roberta.

"Doctor Faux's surgical technique is irrevocable," Mollet answers.

"Are you sure?" asks Roberta hopefully.

"Yes," Mollet says with certainty.

"Then there is no hope at all for Roberta," says Jasmine.

"I'm sorry. Very sorry. If Doctor Faux was here now, he would tell you that even he would not be able to reverse what he had done to you," Mollet says with regret.

"What ever, you might feel. Doctor Faux might have found a way to make a man out of me again," says Roberta with reason.

"No, that is not possible. Ms. Anthony, you must adjust to living as a woman. It should be easy for you. You are young and very womanly. You are beautiful with a perfect body. No one could ever detect that you were once a man. You will be able to function as a woman in every way. Sexually, you will have all the orgasms you want and you can never get pregnant," Doctor Mollet says this with honesty and encouragement.

"Yes. Of course. I understand," says Roberta now feeling that her guts were being torn up inside of her by Molett's diagnosis. She wishes she were dead.

Jasmine, is very disappointed with the doctor's opinion. She just wants to break down and cry but she holds back her tears.

Roberta turns to Jasmine. "It's time to go Jasmine," says Roberta, smiling to hide her disappointment.

Jasmine can see that Roberta's smile is hiding a deep hurt. She takes hold of Roberta's hand.

"Wait," says Mollet.

Roberta and Jasmine stop in their tracks.

"Ms. Anthony, I am so sorry that I could not help you. I hope you can find a way to live with what you can never erase. So I advise you to except what you are. Do not dwell on your past life", says doctor Mollet with sincere, sage advice.

"Yes, I'm aware of all of that. I have a lot of thinking to do," Roberta blurts out unhappily.

THE FIRST LADY

"Of course, and I might be able to help you. Are you free tonight for supper at my place", inquires Doctor Mollet with a flirtatious, devilish smile on his face.

Roberta and Jasmine are stunned by Mollet's insensitive suggestion, after he has just given Roberta a life sentence.

Roberta, ignores his offer and she and Jasmine hurriedly leave the room. They work their way to the front office and exit into the corridor.

Jasmine does not stop and she automatically heads for the elevators. Roberta does not go with her, instead moves to a small bench near a window that overlooks the city.

Jasmine is not aware that Roberta is not with her. She gets to the elevators and turns to say something to Roberta and sees that she is not with her. Jasmine puzzled, looks around to see what has happened to Roberta and sees her collapsed on a bench with her head down, sobbing softly, broken hearted.

Jasmine goes to Roberta quickly. She sits down beside her, cradles Roberta's head and slowly, tenderly, strokes her brow to comfort her. She looks into Roberta's tearful face and wants to break down and cry, but does not. Jasmine stares into her brokenhearted friend's wet eyes. Thoughts of guilt go through, Jasmine's mind blaming herself for Anthony's disastrous change of life. If she had not pursued him, enticed him, pushed and flaunted her body on him, exciting his libido, so that he could not refuse to take her virginity, all this would have not happened to Robert Anthony. It was her selfishness of thinking only of herself, trying to get even with Sheik Seid that all this happened. She asks God to forgive her and promises God she will stay with Roberta for the rest of her life and help her.

Jasmine holding back tears, brushes them from her nose with her finger. She kisses Roberta's forehead. "Roberta, I love you, do not cry. Please do not cry. I will take you to see other doctors who might be able to help us," says Jasmine trying to encourage her forlorn friend.

Roberta, hears what Jasmine has said. She sits up and wipes the tears from her eyes and face with the palm of her hands. "No, it's a waste of time. I believe Mollet, what he's told me. I am, what I am and that's the way it's going to stay," says Roberta slowly with reality and finality.

"Do not say that, Roberta. If doctor Faux did not get buried under all of that snow, maybe he could have figured a way to make you a man again," says Jasmine trying to heal the wounded Roberta.

Roberta expels an ironic low laugh. "I doubt it, my dear, dear friend. My maker did a perfect job for Sheik Seid. I just hope that frozen bastard burns in hell," declares Roberta with anger and hate.

"Yes. Yes and the Sheik too. They both deserve the Devil's wrath." says Jasmine with a vindictive desire for revenge. "I curse them both." states Jasmine hatefully as she springs to her feet.

Roberta closes her eyes to hold back her tears. Then after a moment she opens them slowly and a lonely tear drop rolls down her cheek.

Jasmine is very saddened by Roberta's misery.

Roberta, slowly stands up and wipes the tear from her cheek. She moves to the window and looks up at the blazing sun, then down to the busy city streets. Her eyes take in the signature of Paris, the effigy that rises above the city, 'THE EIFFEL TOWER'. Roberta stares at the tall, iron framework structure and thoughts begin to soar in her mind.

A soft smile comes to Roberta's lips. She turns to, Jasmine. "You know, we haven't eaten any food today. I'm a little hungry," says Roberta still smiling.

Jasmine, is taken by surprise of Roberta's new mood. "That is a good idea. I could use some sustenance in my system. I saw a cafe in the lobby on the other side of the elevators. We can go there," says Jasmine with a little laugh and wondering why, Roberta's flip-flop change from depression to normality.

"Jasmine, how much money do we have left?"

"Enough to last us a few days, after that who knows what," responds Jasmine who starts thinking.

"I see, well instead of the cafe downstairs, I would like to go to the top of the Eiffel Tower and then get something to eat in one of their cafes. It's not far from here, we can walk there," says Roberta with a little smile.

"Well, yes, that is a good idea. I would like to see Paris from the top of the Tower and have lunch there," says Jasmine smiling. But deep inside she is a little suspicious of Roberta's change of attitude.

Thoughts begin to roll through Jasmine's mind, asking herself, "Why has Roberta gone from an extreme depression to this light, up tempo mood." She searches her brain for a reason. Then suddenly it hits her, 'Roberta has planned her demise. She wants to leap off from the top of the Eiffel Tower and end her problem. She had better stay close to Roberta every second just in case it is her plan. If it is, she must try and stop her, no matter what. She looks over to Roberta and throws her a big happy smile to cover up her suspicious feelings about her.

"Well, let's get moving before the afternoon sightseers crowd the cafes in there," says Roberta with a small laugh.

Roberta and Jasmine move to the elevators, Jasmine pushes the down button.

"You know Jasmine when I was looking for work as an actor and if I heard they were looking to cast an actor to play a woman, I would have begged to play the part. Now that I am a female I'd give anything to play a man," says Roberta laughing ironically.

An elderly couple, join them at the elevator just as the 'down red light' rings on. The doors to the elevator open and Roberta and Jasmine step aside for the elderly pair. Then they follow them in with the doors closing behind them. Their elevator starts down, as the 'up green light' of the other elevator rings on.

The doors of the up elevator open and two pretty women speaking to each other in French step out of the car first, followed by several other passengers. They all move away going in different direction of the corridor. The last two riders that come out of the elevator are Tufa and Acmen, Sheik Seid's two hit men.

The doors of the elevator close behind Tufa and Acmen and they just stand there looking around and up and down the corridor. Acmen sees something and points to it. "Tufa. Doctor Faux's office," says Acmen excitedly in Arabic.

"Good. Let us hope that the good doctor can lead us to Anthony and Jasmine," says Tufa ominously in Arabic.

They move towards Doctor Faux's office. They both turn on a warm and friendly smile. Acmen, pulls open the office door and with their warm, friendly smiles they enter the office.

Chapter Eighteen
To Live or Die in Paris

Roberta stands as a stolid figure at the base of the Eiffel Tower listening to Jasmine, who is translating in English what is written in French on the dedication plaque attached to the foot of the tower.

"Eiffel Tower," built by: A. G. Eiffel (1832-1923) engineer designer: A tower of iron framework 984 feet high. Built for the International Exposition of 1889."

Roberta, looks up to the top of the tower and starts to think.

'Huh. Nine hundred and eighty four feet. I wonder how many people jumped or fell off from the top accidentally. Did they feel any pain when they hit the ground. That sure is a long drop. Well I'll soon find out.'

Jasmine getting no response from Roberta, turns to her and sees Roberta with a serious look on her face, staring up to the top of the tower. Jasmine hopes Roberta is not thinking of what she suspects her of. Roberta, looks over at Jasmine, "You know Jasmine, that's almost as high as the 'Empire State' building."

"I know, I have never seen the skyscraper in person, only in the movies," says Jasmine with a knowing smile.

"Let's go up to the top of the tower and see the whole city of Paris from the highest spot in town," says Roberta.

The Eiffel Tower elevator rises to the top of the tower with Roberta, Jasmine and several other passengers. Most of the trave-ers on board the climbing iron gated car are excited as it rises above the city and viewing it through the iron slats of the elevators gate doors.

Roberta and Jasmine are passive and just smile to each other and to the riders. The rising conveyance reaches the top and the elevator's operator announces in English with a French accent. "Ladies and Gentlemen we have reached the very top of the tower. When you observe the city surrounding the tower please be careful that you do not lean to far over the railing of the tower. After you have finished your stay here at the top if any of you wish to dine there are several cafes in the tower. Thank you for your cooperation and enjoy the view of Paris." The operator opens the elevators iron gates and the excited passengers spill out of the car and move quickly to the railing around the tower.

Roberta and Jasmine are the last to come out of the elevator. Roberta moves to a section of the iron railing with Jasmine following close behind her. Both of them grab hold of the railing very firmly. They look at each other, smile and lean over the edge of the railing very carefully. The view of the city of Paris from their perspective is colossal and very exciting.

Roberta tilts her head and stares down to the foot of the tower. She studies the distance to the ground and says to herself, "So this is what nine hundred and eighty four feet looks like from up here. Cars and people look like colonies of a crawling army of ants. This is it, Roberta. I'm sorry, but I can't and I won't live the rest of my life as a woman. It all ends here," she laughs ironically to herself. "I know I won't feel any pain when I hit the ground from way up here. I can do this. I must do this. Yes, but I'll have to wait until most of the people leave the top. Then I'll sneak away from Jasmine, then quickly jump."

Jasmine, has been observing Roberta continually staring intently down at the city streets. She now knows deep inside of her that Roberta is making up her mind to end her life. "It is sure a pretty long ways down from here isn't it Roberta?" says Jasmine with a little laugh.

"It sure is," says Roberta laughing to hide her coming intentions.

THE FIRST LADY

Roberta and Jasmine slowly walk around the railing to see the rest of the grand city. They are careful not to bump into any of the other sightseers.

Some of the visitors have circled the top commenting on how beautiful the different parts of Paris look from their view at the top of the Eiffel Tower. They all say they will never forget it as long as they live.

Most of the visitors, have completed their sightseeing and go to the elevator for the trip down. Other visitor's skip the elevator and make their way down the stairways leading to the other floors where there is more to see and various cafes for dinning. Now most of the sightseers have gone except for a young starry-eyed loving couple, who are not aware of Roberta and Jasmine or anyone being present or not.

Roberta and Jasmine have completed their circle around the top of the tower and have seen the exciting busy city of Paris from the height of nine hundred and eighty four feet.

Roberta, thinks now is the time for her to get away from Jasmine and has figured out a way. She turns to Jasmine, "This view of Paris is just spectacular. Aren't you happy we came up here before we left France," says Roberta with verve, really meaning what she has said to Jasmine.

Jasmine has a surprised look on her face. "Yes, yes and the city of Paris even looks more romantic from up here," says Jasmine looking wide-eyed at the city below.

"Well, it's time to leave. I'm really very hungry. Let's go to the cafe at the bottom of the tower," says the feigning Roberta smiling. Jasmine again is surprised and can not figure the change in Roberta.

They start for the elevator and Roberta stops. "Oh, I have to go to the bathroom," says Roberta now playing for time.

"Roberta, you can use the restroom in the cafe," responds Jasmine.

"The elevators aren't here yet. I can't wait. I really have to go now," says Roberta sounding serious.

"Good, then I will go too," says Jasmine who really means it.

They proceed to the restrooms which are on the other side of The elevators. Roberta is about to go into the men's restroom instead of the ladies. "Roberta, that's the men's room," says Jasmine.

"Oh. I forgot," says Roberta laughing and trying to distract Jasmine with humor to hide her forth coming intentions.

They go into the ladies room. Roberta goes into a stall near the exit door of the room and fakes locking the stall door. Jasmine goes into another stall locking her door.

Roberta, as she takes off her shoes. "You know Jasmine this toilet is very comfortable," says Roberta laughing to cover up the sound of her pushing the stall door open.

"It is not too bad for a structure made of iron," says Jasmine who laughs at her joke.

Roberta exits the stall in a flash and is out of the restroom very quietly.

She moves away from the restrooms quickly and looking around the parapet to see if the two love birds are still there or anyone else.

Jasmine, comes out of her stall and goes to the sink to wash her hands. "Roberta, I am finished. I will wait for you outside." Jasmine wipes her hands with a paper towel. She hears no response from Roberta. "Roberta, did you hear what I said?" She gets no answer from Roberta. She then goes to her stall and sees the door is slightly ajar. "Roberta are you alright?" Jasmine hears no answer. She opens the stall door and sees that it is empty then sees Robert's shoes on the floor in front of the toilet bowel. Jasmine immediately knows that Roberta had snuck out of the restroom to get away from her so that she could kill herself by jumping off the tower. Jasmine quickly picks up Roberta's shoes and is out of the ladies room in an instant.

She goes quickly around the top of the tower looking for, Roberta. She gets to the corner of the parapet and sees Roberta on the other side climbing the girder and onto the railing. Jasmine's legs move with speed

as Roberta is about to leap off the tower. "Roberta. Roberta. No. Please stop. Do not do it. Please. Do not kill yourself. I love you Roberta."
screams Jasmine as she rushes to Roberta.

Jasmine's intrusion distracts Roberta and she turns to see Jasmine heading for her. "Jasmine. Please let me die. I can't live like this, I can't and I won't. So please don't make it harder for me." pleads the sobbing Roberta as she turns to jump.

Jasmine, screams, "NO. NO." She drops Roberta's shoes and with all her strength she makes an 'Olympic Gold Medal' broad jump for Roberta's legs as she is about to leap off the tower railing.

Jasmine's jump is just in time. She wraps her arms around Roberta's legs quickly and tightly.

"Jasmine. Let go of me, let me go, let me die," cries the sobbing Roberta, struggling to get her legs free from Jasmine's grip.

"No. if you die, I die with you." shouts the wailing Jasmine. "It is all, my fault Roberta of what Sheik Seid has done to you, my fault. I am the only one that you should blame for what you are now. Your change. Your life. Please do not want to die I will help your new life. Together we can make your new life work. Please Roberta, please," begs the crying Jasmine.

Roberta has been listening and digesting what Jasmine has been saying to her. Her crying begins to subside and slowly she stops trying to get free from Jasmine. Roberta stops struggling.

There is a long silence and with wet eyes Roberta looks down at, Jasmine. "Alright. Alright, Jasmine. I don't want you to die because of what we did together. I'm also to blame for what happened. I could have refused you, but I wanted you just as much you wanted me. So stop blaming yourself. It's been a two way street," confesses Roberta, truthfully.

"Then you will not kill yourself?" asks Jasmine holding her breath.

"No. I will take your advice, and if things get really rough for me to cope with, I may change my mind. So for now Jasmine, I'll give

Roberta a real good try," says Roberta with a little laugh. She wipes her wet eyes and cheeks with the palm of her free hand and still holding on to the girder with the other hand.

Jasmine is releived and satisfied with Roberta's intent. She smiles slowly releasing Roberta's legs. "I know, Roberta will make it and she will live a long, full, happy life. God will see to that. When ever you need him, he will help you cope," says Jasmine with her religious faith.

Roberta comes down to the parapet. Jasmine hugs her very tightly and says, "You are going to be alright now." Jasmine, picks up Roberta's shoes and puts them on her. Roberta wipes her eyes with her hand. She smiles nodding her head to Jasmine and mouths a 'thank you'. Then she and Jasmine move slowly to the elevators just as one elevator comes up to the top floor. The gates open and a dozen sightseers, men and women exit the car.

"How is that for timing Jasmine?" chides Roberta with a smile.

Jasmine laughs as she and Roberta enter the elevator. "Down to the bottom floor cafe, please," says Jasmine smiling to the elevator operator.

"I hope you both have enjoyed the view of the city of Paris from nine hundred and eighty four feet," says the operator, giving them a flirtatious smile.

"It couldn't be better. It gives your self a different perspective of life," says Roberta with an ironic laugh, as does Jasmine. The operator starts the elevator and Roberta and Jasmine go down to the bottom floor of the Eiffel Tower.

Most of the tables on the ground floor cafe in the Eiffel Tower are occupied by people of all ages. Two waiters are serving the patrons. Jasmine spots an empty table and she and Roberta approach it and sit down. Across from them is a man in his fifties who is eating by himself. The man sees them and gives them a big friendly smile. Roberta smiles back to the man and so does Jasmine who gives the man a friendly toss of her head.

A busy waiter comes over to Roberta and Jasmine's table, hands them a menu and moves off to help other customers at tables nearby. Jasmine scans the menu. "They have a lot of good dishes. But very expensive."

"Jasmine, maybe we can afford the French omelet with a croissant," suggests Roberta.

"Yes, we can, but we have to split it," advises Jasmine.

The man smile to them again. Roberta smiles back to him.

"You know, I think that man is trying to pick us up," says Jasmine smiling back at him. "I have a feeling that things are going to be alright for us," says Jasmine hopefully.

"I hope so, but right now all I want to do is get back to America and see my Aunt Bea, to let her know that Roberta is still alive. I mean Robert. Oh damn it, Jasmine, I'm so mixed up," says Roberta flustered.

Jasmine touches Roberta's arm to comfort her.

"Well, I'll tell her what happened to me and I just hope, she'll understand," says Roberta hopefully.

"She will," Jasmine presses Roberta's hand.

"Shit, what the hell am I talking about. We don't even have plane fare, to get to the America. I can't even go to the U. S. Embassy for help. I don't want them know to what happened to me. I don't want anyone to know, except my Aunt Bea," says Roberta with moist eyes.

"I agree, Roberta. Look, maybe we can get enough money for one ticket to America. I can stay here after I tell the French what has happened to me, I know they would grant me political asylum. Then I can find a job and save money for a plane ticket and join you," says Jasmine who is being very sincere and very practical.

"Forget it Jasmine, we've come a long way together and if it weren't for you, I would have rotted in Sheik Kassem's Harem for the rest of my miserable life and you talked me out of deep sixing myself. No, no, I'm not going to leave you here. You're coming back to the U. S. with me. In America with your degree you can find a job. We'll find the money some where," Roberta is firm in her response. They hug each other.

Roberta and Jasmine are almost in tears. When they have regained their composure Roberta notices that the smiling man who is sitting at the table across from them is now staring at them, grinning.

Roberta is annoyed at the grinning man. "That smiling guy at the table across from us is now staring and grinning at us. I wish the hell he would stop," says Roberta a little annoyed.

"He probably thinks we are ladies of the night," chuckles Jasmine.

"Maybe that's the only way to get the plane fare for the trip," Roberta puts her hand over her mouth to stop what she was saying and then continues. "What the hell am I saying, I must be flipping my lid," Roberta starts to untie her thoughts and thinks sanely.

Jasmine lets out a little laugh. "No Roberta, you are just starting to think like a woman. Many would resort to that to survive," the wise Jasmine adds.

"Well, right now I'm a little too young to sleep with a man. I'm only eight months old," Roberta mimics like a little girl. Jasmine bursts out into laughter, Roberta joins in.

The grinning man thinks that they were laughing at him so he signals for the waiter for the bill. The waiter comes and hands the man the bill. The man pays his bill and gives the waiter a big tip.

"Thank you mister Vilar," the waiter speaks in French. Vilar gets out of his chair and approaches Roberta and Jasmine. When he does Roberta and Jasmine stop laughing. Vilar smiles then takes a business card out of his wallet.

"Ladies," says Vilar in a French accent smiling and bowing his head slightly. "I am Edgar Vilar, a theatrical agent, may I sit down?" asks the affable Frenchman.

THE FIRST LADY

Roberta and Jasmine looked at each other curiously. They both hesitate, look at each other again and then gesture for him to sit down.

As he sits down he hands his business card to Roberta.

Vilar, wastes no time. "I have three clients working in a movie that is presently being filmed here. It is an American French co-production," says Vilar in a business-like fashion.

"But, Mr. Vilar, what is this all got to do with us?" says Roberta suspiciously.

The well mannered Frenchmen is gracious, understanding. He smiles. "Well, you see Madame, ah," starts Vilar.

"Mr. Vilar my name is Mann, Roberta Mann. This is my good friend and companion, ah, Jas, Mary," Roberta is a little tongue tied and smiles, enjoying this female test.

"Yes. Mary, Mary Sabah," Jasmine jumps in with a smile.

"Yes good to meet you both. You see, I have been trying to find a beautiful American woman for a small role in this picture. It is a part of an American girl who is stranded in Paris."

Roberta and Jasmine look at each other stunned, but try to hide it with innocent girlish looks.

"And she needs the money to get back to the United States," explains Vilar.

"Is that right," Roberta is smiling to Jasmine.

"Yes, the director is ready to use a French girl and dub her voice in American. But he would not like to do that because it is a true story," says Vilar.

"I'll bet it is," Roberta is devilish. She winks at the smiling Jasmine.

"Yes. So when I saw how beautiful you are and heard you speak American, I knew I found Shannon, the American who sells her body for money to buy a plane ticket to America." Vilar is so happy and proud that he had found the right girl for the film.

"You want me to play a hooker?" Roberta asks with a playful smile on her face.

Jasmine bites her tongue to keep from laughing. Instead she smiles boldly and winks back at Roberta. "Mr. Vilar, how much would a part like that pay Roberta?" inquires Jasmine whose interest is in the amount they need to get to the U.S.

"Five hundred American dollars for a days work and an extra one hundred dollars because the roles calls for nudity in the scene," says the agent without batting an eye.

Roberta is not shocked because she knew that actors and actresses had to do what the script called for and what the director wanted. If you want the job, you do it. If not, you walk. But in Roberta's case she is not sure she could go naked in front of the whole world, she hesitates.

Jasmine is not shocked either. She smiles, leans over to Roberta and whispers in her ear. "I know what you are thinking and how you must feel, but you are a beautiful woman. No one can ever change that and you must think as a woman. You have a beautiful body, do not be ashamed to show it. Now tell the man you want more money." Jasmine's Arab business sense knew that Vilar will get Roberta more money because they needed an American girl to play the scene.

Roberta thinks for a moment. After all she knows that Jasmine is right and that they need as much money as she can get. Enough to buy two plane fares, home. Roberta smiles and nods her head in agreement to Jasmine. She knew what she had to say to Vilar would be hard for her. So she gives the French agent a girlish smile, takes a deep breath and clears her throat. "Mr. Vilar, alright, I'll do the nude scene, but, I want more money," Roberta puts it coldly.

"Well, how much more do you want?" asks Vilar smiling.

"I want, fifteen hundred dollars," says Roberta very calmly.

"Mon Dieu. That is impossible. They will not pay that much. But he hesitates. I think I can get you one thousand dollars and I will forgo my commission," says Vilar holding his breath.

Roberta looks over to Jasmine who nods her head to her. "Mr. Vilar, you have a deal. By the way, who is the American producer?" asks Roberta sounding very professional.

"Joe Canin from Hollywood," replies Vilar smiling.

Roberta and Jasmine are stunned when they hear that Joe Canin is the American producer of the film. How ironic, Robert Anthony was at Joe Canin's grand Hollywood party where he met Jasmine and was kidnapped that night by Sheik Seid, which is now a short story.

Vilar takes out another business card from his wallet and scribbles something on the back of his card. "Now, this is the address of the shooting location. Be there at six A.M. ," says Vilar giving the card to Roberta who is just recovering from his proposition.

"Well, what if the director and this Canin guy don't think I'm right for the part?" Roberta says as an excuse for her slow response.

"Like you, they both will be thrilled when they see you," says Vilar with a sensual smile on his face.

Roberta had an "Oh Shit" look on her face, she hopes Joe Canin doesn't recognize her or Jasmine.

Jasmine is not apprehensive because she knows that they would never recognize Robert Anthony's new look. As far as she is concerned, she did not give a crap if Joe Canin did recognize her. So what. She gives Roberta, a confident look and giggles.

"Roberta, I do not think you will have a problem. They will love a new face in the role, a beautiful face, with a beautiful body," says Jasmine making Roberta understand that she will never be recognized in her new suite of clothes.

WILLIAM HELLINGER

Roberta gets Jasmine's message. But as far as Roberta was concerned the jury is still out.

Chapter Nineteen
The Sheik's Hit Men

The doors to one of the Lafayette Medical building elevators, opens spilling its passengers out into the busy lobby. Tufa and Acmen are among them. With concerned looks on they faces, they head for the exit to the boulevard. Aomen sees several telephone booths at the other side of the spacious modern lobby. Most of them are occupied. He nudges Tufa, points to the booths and they move quickly to them. Tufa steps into an empty booth and closes the door. Acmen, stands outside the door on guard.

Tufa pulls a small cell phone and his wallet out of an inside pocket of his jacket. Carefully he dials a mass of numbers on the cell phone. He waits, then he hears the ringing of the phone on the other end.

After the three rings the phone is finally answered.

"Office of Sheik Seid, the Oil Minister of Bokuf. How can I help you?" says a female voice in Arabic.

"This is Tufa," says Tufa. I wish to speak with my Sheik," says Tufa with urgency in Arabic.

"Yes, Tufa, the Sheik has been expecting your call. Hold a moment," says the cordial female voice.

Tufa presses the phone to his ear and waits, and waits. Finally he hears the voice of the Sheik on the other end.

"Yes, Tufa," says the Sheik in Arabic.

"My Sheik, Doctor Faux, is dead," says Tufa as the Sheik cuts in.

"What?" says the shocked Sheik.

"Yes. Doctor Faux, is dead. Another doctor, a Doctor Mollet has taken over his practice, he told us that three months ago Doctor Faux was climbing up Mt. Everest when an avalanche killed him and the group he was climbing with," says Tufa.

"I see. Well that is too bad," says the Sheik a little sad. But he gets over the sadness very quickly.

"Tufa, what about Anthony and Jasmine?" asks the Sheik with anticipation.

"Doctor Mollet said that Anthony and Jasmine came to his office yesterday. He examined Anthony and told her no one else could reverse doctor Faux's surgery. she is stuck with her body," reports Tufa.

"That makes me very, very happy," declares the Sheik with joy.

"My Sheik. It seems that Anthony and Jasmine have not left Paris, so they must still be here," says Tufa.

"Alright you and Acmen find them. No matter where they are. I know one thing Tufa a they will eventually go back to America. Hollywood California. If in one week you are unable to find them, go there." says the Sheik with a vengeance in his voice.

"Yes, my Sheik, we will do as you command. I know we will find them and when we do, we will destroy them," says Tufa who is gung ho.

"Good. May Allah be with you both." says the Sheik. Seid knew that Tufa and Acmen will do his bidding.

Tufa hears the Sheik hang up on the other end. With a sweaty hand Tufa snaps off the cell phone and puts it back into his breast pocket. He thinks a moment, hoping that he can do his Sheik's bidding. He sighs and then opens the phone booth door and gives Acmen a big Arab smile with a nervous twitch of his mouth.

Chapter Twenty
A Star is Born

The Left Bank apartment houses overlook all of the historic buildings in the area. The early morning traffic is very thin and the only pedestrians on the street at that time of the morning are people walking to work.

A large apartment bedroom in one of the Left Bank apartment houses is alive and buzzing with a French movie crew, who are converting the room into a sound stage. The camera man is floating around the room checking the lights with his light meter.

A man of forty, Marcel Racine the director of the film is in a huddle with producer Joe Canin. The assistant director a young man in his twenties comes into the bedroom from the living room and goes directly to Canin and Racine.

"Marcel, the American girl is ready for you," says Francois in French.

"Good, Francois," answers Marcel in French.

"I must say, Marcel, Vilar has great taste. Roberta Mann is beautiful," says Canin excitedly in English.

"Yes she is, and with a magnificent body. Thank God," replies Marcel in English with a French accent, who was very pleased with the casting. "Alright, Francois, let us make it," declares Marcel in French.

"Attention, everyone. Get to your positions. We are going to roll," shouts Francois in French.

The camera man and his crew get to their positions and quickly check their equipment. Canin moves into the living room with Francois following him.

In the living room Roberta is dressed in a very sexy dress. Nearby is a handsome middle aged French actor who is dressed in designers pajamas. A make-up man and wardrobe girl move to them and do a last minute check-up on both of them.

Jasmine is sitting on the couch drinking a cup of coffee, she gives Roberta an encouraging and confident smile. Roberta smiles back nervously.

Canin approaches Roberta. Francois walks over to the French actor and says something in French to the man. The actor smiles, and starts for the bedroom with Francios following him.

"Miss Mann, the director is ready to shoot your scene. I know this may be just a small part, but it's a very important one. I understand that this is all new to you, so I don't want you to be nervous," Canin speaks with a confident smile.

"I'll try not to, Mr. Canin," says Roberta with a girlish giggle. "I'll just have to make believe that this is really happening to me," says Roberta with naivete.

"Good. You just sounded like one of those method actors," says Canin laughing.

"Oh. I didn't know that, what a coincidence," Roberta says with another girlish giggle.

"Yes," says Canin with a big smile. "and Miss Mann, when you get to L.A. I want you to look me up," says Canin smiling sensually.

"I will, but only if you like me in the scene," replies Roberta who is flapping her false eyelashes and smiling broadly.

"Miss Mann, I have a feeling you will do Good," says Canin smiling and now looking over at Jasmine, "Miss Sabah are you sure we never met before?" says Canin trying to recollect.

"Oh I am positive, if I did I would have remembered you," says Jasmine flirtatiously and smiling.

Canin smiles broadly and Roberta turns and coughs to keep from laughing.

Francois' head appears in the open door-way of the bedroom.

"Miss Mann, we are ready for you now," Francois says in English in his French accent.

"Thank you," says Roberta giving the assistant director a big smile. Just then a sound man goes past Francois. He is harnessed with portable sound equipment with a small boom and microphone attached to it. He takes a position near Roberta.

Roberta now tense begins to prepare herself for her cue to say her lines. She says to herself, "How ironic all this is. Robert Anthony the actor, is no more, now Roberta Mann is working in a bit role in a French film, as an actress. Roberta will say her lines, get paid, go back to America and see if she wants to live the rest of her life as a woman or put myself out of my misery." She sighs and looks over to Jasmine. The young Arab sees Roberta's tension, smiles and gives her a good-luck sign. Jasmine then follows Canin into the bedroom.

In the bedroom set the director and crew are in their positions ready to start shooting the first take of the bedroom scene. The French actor is already in the bed, he has the bed covers pulled up to his shoulders. His eyes are closed as if he is asleep.

At that moment, Laval the French producer comes into the bedroom, "Gentlemen, I am sorry I am late. I had to get the French Actors Guild's approval to hire Miss Anthony," Laval speaks in good English with a very slight French accent. Marcel smiles to Laval acknowledging him. The producer then takes a position alongside of Canin. Canin gave his co-producer a thankful pat on his back.

Everyone is in place and Francois gives the ready sign with his hand to Racine and the director motions to his assistant.

"Alright, quiet on the set," orders Francois in French. Suddenly the bedroom set becomes quiet as a tomb.

"Action," commands Racine in French.

"Roll Sound, take one," shouts Francois.

Cue door chimes," says Racine.

"DOOR, CHIMES. GO." declares Francois.

Immediately, the sound of the door chimes is heard as though they were coming from the front door of the apartment. The closed eyes of the actor in the bed, blinks slightly. After a moment, the sound of the door chimes is heard again coming from the apartment's front door. This time the actors' eyes flip open and he springs quickly out of the bed and hurries into the living room.

Racine waits in anticipation. He hears the sound of the front door of the apartment opening and closing, then after a moment he hears, Roberta's character say, "Mr. Leon?" "Yes," replies the actor playing the character of Leon in English.

Racine holds his breath as he listens to the rest of the scene, hoping that the actors do not blow their lines.

"I'm Shannon. Mr. Pascal sent me," says Roberta's character Shannon ever so sweetly.

"I know he called me. He told me how beautiful you are. Yes. Yes, he was right Shannon," says the actors character Leon.

"Did he tell you how much I want?" asks Roberta's character Shannon.

"Yes, $500 American dollars," replies Leon the actors' character.

"Then it's okay," says Roberta's character Shannon.

Francois signals for the camera operator to roll the camera. The man quickly flips the camera switch on and frames and focuses the camera on the door of the bedroom. The actor playing Leon comes into the bedroom. The camera picks up Roberta playing Shannon as she follows the actors character Leon into the bedroom.

The actors character Leon then crosses to the night table as the camera follows him. He opens the drawer of the night table, pulls out some American money, counts out five one hundred dollar bills. He gives the money to the character Shannon who puts the money into her hand bag.

"You know, I have never done this before," says the actors character Leon with a nervous smile.

"Neither have I," replies Roberta's character Shannon smiling.

The actors character Leon looks at Roberta's character Shannon with surprise.

It was now time for Shannon Roberta's character to strip off her clothes. Roberta hesitates, but not in the character of Shannon she is portraying, but as Roberta herself for everyone in the room. "Well this is it," Roberta says to herself. "Can I really strip off all my clothes and go through with this heavy sex scene with this man? What do I do. God help me. Please God, if I don't go through with this, I will have to kill myself. I don't want to die. Please God, give me the strength to live as a woman." Roberta's eyes scan the room, they stare into the faces of the director, the crew and all who are anticipating the disrobing of Roberta Mann.

Roberta sees the pleading in the eyes of Jasmine. That's when she makes her decision to try to live as a woman. So to keep up with her act Roberta imagines she can hear strip music. A soft, sensual smile comes over Roberta's face and slowly, she begins to peel off her clothes.

Racine, Canin, the actor playing Leon, the crew and even Jasmine, watch Roberta with full expectation as she undresses and displays her beautiful body.

WILLIAM HELLINGER

Now, Roberta's character Shannon is naked as she gets into bed with Leon.

The scene is hot and heavy. The camera picks up the two sweaty bodies in the bed that are engulfed in sex. Roberta's character Shannon and the actor's character Leon, are making mad, movie, sensual love. The scene look very real.

When Jasmine sees how Roberta is acting in the sex scene she knows at once, that Roberta is going to be okay. That she was going to make it as a woman, a full fledged, beautiful, sensual, female.

When the camera moves in for a close-up of the two writhing bodies in the bed, Racine has a sensual smile on his face he watches Roberta and the actor playing the sex scene with so much realism. It also appears that the director must have got an erection. Racine waits a few moments, and then yells, "Cut."

Roberta smiles and pulls the bed covers over her naked body. Jasmine gives Roberta a high sign that she was great and moves to her.

"Roberta, you were marvelous," says Canin.

"Absolutely, beautiful," says Laval in English. Jasmine is bursting with joy shaking her head "yes," to her dear friend Roberta.

The last frame of Roberta's sex scene is just ending in a screening room in Paris the next day. Everyone in the room was engrossed in the scene except Roberta who is a little embarrassed. Jasmine is holding Roberta's hand tightly to give her encouragement.

When the lights in the screening room come up there is an excited hub bub in the room. Racine moves to Roberta. "You were magnificent, suburb, both of you were terrific. I loved it," declares the director. "Roberta, you were so good I have decided to enlarge the part of Shannon." He pauses and looks around, "That's if the producers agree with me."

"Yes, it works for me," says Canin.

"I would insist, Marcel," says Laval.

"Then it is settled. By tomorrow I will have your new scenes written," says Racine.

"That sounds good. I just hope you won't be disappointed in me," says Roberta as she looks over to Jasmine smiling.

"You will be fine. Your character will give this story a shot in the arm," Racine informs her with assurance.

"Oh, and of course you'll be paid more money," Canin says.

"Yes, your agent Vilar will be informed," adds Laval.

"Good, could you also include two first class fares to the United States?" Roberta says winking to Jasmine.

Canin and Laval look at each other in query. They both smile and nod their heads in agreement.

Chapter Twenty-One
Home Again

A French passenger jet moves quickly through the sky. L.A.X is ahead of them as the jet starts its slow descent.

Roberta and Jasmine are sitting in the first class seats of the French jet. They see the 'Fasten Seat Belts' sign flash on. And they snap on their seat belts. Roberta looks out of the jet's window by her seat. She sees the city of Los Angeles below her.

"We're approaching LAX. Jasmine, we made it." Roberta is now with a happy smile and a sigh of relief. "Home again, thank God?"

Jasmine leans over and looks out of Roberta's window seat. "Los Angeles still looks the same from the air from when I saw it the first time, Roberta. It is such a big city," Jasmine states with an, 'I'm home, too smile.'

A baggage man comes out of the L.A.X. terminal building wheeling a baggage cart with four pieces of luggage on it. Roberta and Jasmine are close behind the cart. The baggage man hails a cab for Roberta and Jasmine. Lucky enough a taxi driver sees the baggage man's signal. Roberta and Jasmine get into the back seat of the cab. The driver loads their luggage in the trunk of his taxi, gets into his cab and drives off into the traffic.

The taxi driver looked into his rear view mirror. "Where to, Ladies?" he inquires.

"North Hollywood, 12684 Ensign," Roberta says excitingly. "You got it. I know the area quite well. Get comfortable it's a long ride this time in the morning," says the cabby smiling in his rear view mirror.

"Roberta, Aunt Bea, she might not be in. You should have called her," says Jasmine concerned.

"She's home, Jasmine. I just want to surprise her and Sam," says Roberta knowingly.

"Yes, are they going to be surprised," says Jasmine in an ominous tone of voice.

Of course Aunt Bea is home, she is in the back yard raking up leaves. Sam is lying nearby.

Aunt Bea's face looks drawn and her enthusiasm is gone. She really doesn't care if the leaves were picked up or not. She is just trying to keep herself busy. She thinks of Robert every minute of the day. It's over eight months since Robert is missing. Robert is her nephew but she raised him like the child missing and raised him like the child she never had.

She will never get over Robert until the day she dies.

Roberta and Jasmine's taxi pulled up to Aunt Bea's house. Roberta pays the cab driver. "Cabby, could you wait," says Roberta now a little apprehensive.

"Roberta. Now is not the time to freeze," says Jasmine touching her with encouragement.

"That's easy for you to say. Oh Jasmine, I'm so afraid to face Aunt Bea. What she might say to me. I, I," says Roberta with moist eyes.

"What can she say Roberta. Except that Robert is alive. That is what really counts to her. Everything else is Camel turd, so let us go, I want to meet the woman who raised you," says Jasmine as she gives Roberta a warm touch for strength and courage.

THE FIRST LADY

Roberta and Jasmine got out of the taxi. The cab driver unloads their luggage at the curb. Roberta turns to the driver. "You can go cabby, thanks." The driver smiles and drives off.

Roberta goes to the front door of the house, Jasmine is following close behind her. Roberta hesitates for a moment then she pushes the front door bell, it rings loudly.

Aunt Bea doesn't hear the sound of the front door bell, nor does Sam. Roberta rings the door bell two more times. Now Sam hears it and starts to bark. He runs to the fence and leaps barking excitedly. Aunt Bea drops the rake, "I'm coming. I'm coming. Just hold on," shouts Aunt Bea. Bea, quickly moves into the house with Sam right behind her.

She comes into the living room with a frisky barking Sam alongside of her. The dog rushes to the front door, leaping and jumping on it.

"Quiet Sam, you'll frighten them away. Let's see who it is first. Then if we don't like them, you can bark your head off at them and they'll go away. Okay Sam?" says Aunt Bea.

Sam stops barking immediately and he sits with nervous anticipation and friendliness.

Aunt Bea opens the door. She sees Roberta and Jasmine through the locked screen door, their suitcases on the ground beside them. "Yes," says Aunt Bea.

"Aunt Bea, we're very good friends of your nephew Robert," says Roberta a little nervous.

"Robert? Oh, where is he? Where is he?" says Aunt Bea very excitedly. She unlocks the screen door quickly. Sam just sits there with his tail wagging a mile a minute, then stretches his head out to the two woman, sniffing them.

"Oh, when is my Robert coming home," says Aunt Bea happy and even more excited.

Roberta and Jasmine pick up their suitcases, come into the living room and set their luggage down on the floor of the small room.

With a big happy smile, Aunt Bea closes the front door. Sam moves to Roberta and sits at her feet.

"Who ever you both are, please tell me when Robert will be coming home," says Aunt Bea with happy tears.

Roberta looks over to Jasmine. Jasmine, smiles and motions to Roberta to let her Aunt Bea know who she is.

"Robert is home, Aunt Bea," says Roberta in a tender sweet tone of voice.

"What? Where?" says Aunt Bea, puzzled.

Roberta smiles then moves to her Aunt Bea and hugs her. Jasmine has a big smile of approval on her face.

"What's going on here." says Aunt Bea very confused.

Sam, head cocked pushes himself in between Roberta and Aunt Bea. Sam begins to whine as he knows that Roberta is Robert.

Aunt Bea looks into Roberta's eyes for a long moment and a soft smile comes to her now, calm face. "Yes. It is you Robert. But what have you done to yourself," says Aunt Bea with tears running down her confused face.

Roberta hugs her Aunt Bea very tightly to comfort her. "Aunt Bea, please don't cry. Everything is going to be alright now that I'm home," says Roberta with a soft whispering sweet smile as she holds up the tearful face of her Aunt Bea. Roberta kisses her aunt's face and hugs her tightly again, then she looks over to Jasmine with a sigh of relief and a smile.

Night clouds float pass a bright full moon that casted a shadow of light on Aunt Bea's house. The only lights that are on in the house are in Aunt Bea's dining room.

Roberta and Jasmine are seated at the dining room table finishing their last bite of dinner that Aunt Bea had cooked for them. Sam is under the table lying at Roberta's feet, happy and content.

Aunt Bea, comes in from the kitchen carrying a tray with three coffee cups, a coffee pot and three desert plates with a large piece of Aunt Bea's home made peach pie.

"There it is Jasmine, Aunt Bea's home made peach pie. Wait till you taste it, you'll never want to eat another Baklava again," says Roberta with a happy laugh.

Aunt Bea smiling sets the tray on the table and places the peach pie in front of Roberta and Jasmine. She pours the coffee into the cups and sets them next to her home made pie.

Roberta and Aunt Bea hold their breath. Jasmine let the home made pie slide down her throat and as it does, she let out a happy moaning sound.

"Didn't I tell you she makes the greatest peach pie in the world," declares Roberta proudly.

With a content smile Jasmine nods her head and then takes another piece of the pie into her mouth. "Oh, Aunt Bea you must sell your pies, it is the best I have ever eaten," says Jasmine swallowing down the piece of pie with gusto.

"No, I could never sell them. I only enjoy making them for Rob, Rob. Roberta. Oh, that terrible Arab Sheik. Forgive me. I've just got to get use to you being around as a woman," says Aunt Bea almost apologetically.

"You will Aunt Bea, especially when you see the part that Roberta plays in the picture she made in France," says Jasmine with a big smile.

"Oh, I can't wait Roberta. I remember when you were small. You were a beautiful little thing, with long red hair. People use to think you were a little girl," Aunt Bea has a happy smile

"Really Aunt Bea? You're not just making that up," Roberta asks inquisitively.

"It's true. You were very beautiful and even more so now ," says Aunt Bea who begins to cry.

Roberta goes to her Aunt and puts her arms around her lovingly. "Aunt Bea. It's still me. Only now, I'm your niece Roberta. You can tell your friends and neighbors that your niece from back East is staying with you," says Roberta smiling.

"Yes, oh, yes, I've always wanted to have a niece and now I have one," Aunt Bea kisses Roberta on the cheek.

Jasmine sees that Roberta's smile turned into a mask of compliance.

Jasmine knows now that Roberta has accepted her new life as a woman, because her Aunt Bea has accepted her nephew Robert as her niece Roberta. Smiling with happiness, Jasmine gives Roberta a sign of good luck for a happy life as a woman.

Chapter Twenty-Two
Roberta Mann Movie Star

Tufa and Acmen are standing by the newspaper rack at the Hollywood International newsstand. They are both reading different dated copies of their home town newspaper 'The Arab Daily'.

"Acmen, listen to this." says Tufa in Arabic reading from the paper. "It is rumored that Bokuf's Oil Minister Sheik Seid, is being investigated by the Prime Minister and King Jamal's advisers. It is believed that the Oil Minister has been skimming some money from oil profits into a secret bank account. Sheik Seid denies the allocations and can prove his innocence. In the meanwhile, until further investigation Sheik Seid will remain Oil Minster."

"Someone must be trying to make trouble for our Sheik. I do not believe what they are saying about him," says Acmen with concern.

"Neither do I, our Sheik is innocent," says Tufa with anger.

"Yes, may Allah be with him," declares Acmen looking up into the heavens and mumbling a prayer for his Sheik.

Tufa approaches the news man and pays him for the two Arab papers. He is about to join Acmen but his eyes catch a picture of Roberta on the front page of THE DAILY VARIETY. He grabs a copy of the theatrical newspaper, pays the news man and goes quickly to Acmen. "Look, it is a picture of Roberta Anthony," says Tufa surprised.

"Yes it is, but the name underneath her picture is Roberta Mann," says Acmen a little puzzled.

"Of course. Look what the headlines say." "CANIN PIX HIT. ROBERTA MANN HIS NEW FIND, MARVELOUS & BEAUTIFUL," says Tufa in English.

"Mmm. Roberta has become a movie star. She should not be hard to find," says Acmen also in English with a dirty laugh.

Tufa begins to read the text under Roberta's picture. "Joe Canin will be having a sit-down dinner party honoring Roberta Mann his new find. It will be given at his Beverly Hills estate on the evening of August 1st. Everybody who is anybody in Hollywood has been invited," says Tufa with an evil grin on his face.

"Tufa. Aug 1st is Saturday," says Acmen.

"We will be there and we will do our Sheik's bidding," declares Tufa ominously. "We will call the Sheik tonight, this news will make him feel better," says Tufa with a happy smile.

"Tufa, the gun, the knife, or a plastic bag," says Acmen with a look of joy on his face.

"Whatever, we will have to use, Acmen. So we will take them all," says Tufa with an anxious tone in his voice. It is now Saturday, August 1st, 8:00 P.M. Tufa and Acmen pull up to the curb and park their car across the street from the Canin Mansion. They see that the lights are on in the big house and around the grounds. They notice the tall wrought iron front gates are closed and flanked by walls that encircled the property.

"Acmen, we should have no problems getting on to the property. Roberta is there, we will dispose of her," says Tufa with glee.

"Yes, and where Roberta is, so is Jasmine," says Acmen with ironic laughter.

They get out of the car and walk to the far end of the wall, where there is an oak tree with its heavy branches extending to the edge of the barrier. Acmen helps Tufa up the tree. When Tufa gets to the edge of the

THE FIRST LADY

wall he helps Acmen up. Carefully Tufa and Acmen climb over the wall and drop onto the property.

Staying in the shadows they slowly work their way toward the back of the property.

The Canin dining room is ornately furnished. Elegantly dressed guests, young and middle age men and women are seated around a long dining room table. Most of the crowd run the movie industry in Hollywood and Internationally.

Joe Canin is sitting at the head of the table. Roberta is to his right and next to her is Raymond Lovel, a good-looking man in his early forties. Lovel is the governor of South Dakota and he is a possible presidential candidate for his political party.

Ellen and Harry Stuart are seated on the other side of Roberta. Aunt Bea is sitting next to Jasmine who is seated to the left of Diana Canin. They sit at the other end of the long table.

Roberta and Jasmine look beautiful. They are dressed in lovely Gucci gowns, as is Aunt Bea, who looks so happy. She is bursting with pride. On occasion she looks over to her niece Roberta and gives her a big smile.

Dinner has just been concluded and six uniformed waiters, three men and three women are now serving the dinner guests champagne. The room is filled with sounds of chatter by the guests.

A large five tier whip cream cake with an American and French flag surrounding it is wheeled in on a cart by a chubby man dressed as a baker. The crowd goes wild with 'Oooh's and Aaah's'. On top of the culinary art is a nude female, a shapely, beautiful long red headed doll under an arch that's over the adorned cake.

Attached to the arch is the title of Canin's movie, "THE EMBRACE." The room suddenly becomes silent, then everyone begins to applaud Joe Canin.

Canin gets up from his chair and raises his hand for silence. The room gets quiet quickly.

"I want to thank all of you for coming here tonight. As you all know, 'The Embrace' is a smash. The artists, the American and French production crews, made all this possible. This party tonight is honoring one of the actors. My new find, the beautiful and talented Roberta Mann. She is going to star in my next film, "The Perfect Woman," declares Canin with great pride and joy. Canin then signals for Roberta to stand up.

Roberta is overwhelmed as she slowly gets up from her chair with a big smile. Everyone applauds her. She looks over to Jasmine and her Aunt Bea who are both smiling from ear to ear.

Canin picks up his glass of champagne. "A toast of good luck to the beautiful, Roberta Mann," says Canin above the din of the crowd. Roberta gives Canin a big nervous smile.

The guests stop applauding, get to their feet and pick up their glasses and all in unison sing out, "Good Luck, Roberta." They drink down their champagne and then sit.

"Now, let's all have a piece of that yummy work of art," says Canin with a proud smile and gesture to the chubby baker.

Everyone laughs at Canin's remark. The baker then began to cut the big cake. The waiters stand by with desert dishes that they retrieve magically from underneath the cart.

Roberta hadn't notice that Raymond Lovel was staring at her with an interested, inquiring look on his handsome face.

"Roberta." Roberta turns to Lovel. "I saw your picture and I thought you were just wonderful," says Lovel with a big smile.

"Thank you Governor Lovel," says Roberta smiling.

"Raymond, please." Lovel flashes Roberta a most handsome smile.

Roberta hesitates, then, "Raymond, it was only a tiny part," says Roberta with a shy smile.

THE FIRST LADY

"Yes, but oh, what a revealing one," smiles Lovel as he stares deeply into Roberta's eyes.

Roberta gives the governor a nervous giggle and as she is about to answer him a waiter comes to them carrying a tray with slices of the cake on dishes. The waiter serves them and moves off.

"Raymond, I want you to know that the critics said the same thing about my nudity," says Roberta smiling as she plants her fork into the slice of cake, picks up a piece and eats it.

"No I wasn't referring to that. I meant, the part that you were playing. Of all that you had to resort to because you were stranded in France," says Lovel with a little laugh.

"Hum. That's good Raymond," says Roberta with an ironic smile.

Diana, is staring at Jasmine intently, with a puzzled look on her face. "Mary, are you sure that we haven't met before," asks Diana.

"Yes, I am sure," replies Jasmine smiling sweetly.

"Hmm, your face is so familiar. I could have sworn that we have met before," says Diana shaking her head in frustration.

"Maybe in another life," says Jasmine with a little laugh.

"No. I don't think so, but it'll come to me," says Diana who was sure of herself. "Oh, Mary, you never told me what you do?," Diana says in a probing tone.

"You see Diana, if you thought I looked familiar, you would have asked me if I were a sex therapist," says Jasmine with a 'Got you smile'.

"You are? Well, I sure could use you and so could some of my lady friends," says Diana sighing.

"Diana, any time. I make house calls and do group sessions," says Jasmine very business like.

"Good, we'll set up an appointment before we leave here tonight. I assure you I can get a good group together," says Diana in a serious tone of voice. Then Diana looks over to Roberta and sees that she is engrossed in a conversation with Lovel. "It seems Roberta is only paying attention to Governor Lovel," says Diana a little catty.

"She must like him," says Jasmine.

"Yes, they make a nice couple," says Aunt Bea smiling.

"They really do, Aunt Bea. Tell me Diana, what do you know about Lovel," inquires Jasmine fishing for information.

"Joe met him when they were shooting a picture in South Dakota. Lovel, is here in Hollywood trying to promote producers to do more productions in his State. His film commission has been very unsuccessful convincing most of them," says Diana.

"He sure is good-looking. Is he married?" asks Aunt Bea. "No he's not," replies Diana

Jasmine is about to say something to Diana, when she sees Roberta and Lovel leave the table and head for the patio-pool area.

"Good. I just hope he is all man," comments Jasmine. Diana is puzzled because she doesn't know how to take Jasmine's remark. Aunt Bea smiles broadly because she knows what Jasmine means.

Tufa and Acmen worked their way to the edge of the patio-pool. The place is well lit, no one is in sight. It is void of guests. Without being detected from their vantage point, they could observe the entire pool-patio area.

"Acmen, let us wait here, for a few moments, then we will move to the back windows of the house, to see where Roberta and Jasmine are," whispers Tufa.

"The night is very warm, Tufa. People may not want to come out of the house," Acmen whispers back.

THE FIRST LADY

"Do not worry, we will kill them tonight. Allah will help us," Tufa now speaks in a low whisper.

Tufa pulls a large switch blade knife out of his pocket. Acmen takes a strangling device out of his back pocket. It is a coiled thin wire, with loops on each end of it. The men look at each other and smile.

Roberta is a little apprehensive as she and Lovel make their way to the patio-pool area. She thought to herself, what if Lovel tries to make a pass at her, what should she do. Should she respond to his advances, or fend him off.

The dilemma is, Roberta as a woman is a 26 year old virgin. But Robert her former self, lost his virginity when he was thirteen and ever since that day, Robert the stud loved women and women loved Robert.

So she will have to follow an over active libido that she had inherited from Robert. Roberta then realizes why she is so confused. She is attracted to Lovel, he is so handsome, sensual looking and if she has to lose her cherry why not to the governor of South. Dakota.

When Roberta and Lovel reach the door to the patio-pool area, Roberta gives Lovel a sensual smile.

"Raymond, I would love a drink, can we get a bottle of champagne to take outside," says Roberta sweetly.

Lovel is a little surprised by Roberta's request. He smiles broadly and bows to her, "Your wish is my command, madam," Lovel gives a happy laugh. He opens the patio-pool door for Roberta graciously.

"I'll find us a nice table near the pool," says Roberta voice trails off as she goes out the door to the patio-pool.

Lovel is happy. He closes the door to the patio-pool and rushes off to get two glasses and a bottle of champagne.

Roberta looks around the patio—pool, while the noise of the party coming from inside the house filters outside. The sounds of the party send Roberta's mind back to the night of the big party when Robert met Jasmine and she made a request to Robert to get a bottle of champagne with two glasses. Then they sat at one of the patio-pool tables, drank the wine and enjoyed each others company.

Roberta, then remembers how Jasmine lusted for Robert. She wanted him to take her virginity that night. Robert tried to resist her request, but he just couldn't fight off his strong sexual drive, especially since she was young, beautiful and had a great body. So Robert took Jasmine to his parked car, where Jasmine got her wish and where Robert met his demise.

Roberta tries to shake those bad memories from her mind. "Well girl," she says to herself, "This is the greatest acting job of all your life, new or old." Roberta laughs ironically, crosses to a table near the edge of the pool and sits in one of the chairs facing the doors to patio-pool.

Tufa and Acmen are surprised and overjoyed when they see that it is Roberta who is sitting at a table not too far from where they were. "Acmen, you stay. I will take care of her. Give me the wire," says Tufa in a low whisper. Acmen nods his head smiling and gives Tufa the deadly wire weapon.

Tufa moves in the shadows of the area, quietly and quickly, towards the unsuspecting Roberta.

Acmen holds his breath as he watches Tufa move closer and closer to his victim.

Roberta is unaware of her assassin. She sits in the chair very relaxed, with her eyes focused on the patio-pool door, waiting for Lovel to come out.

Tufa reaches Roberta and he strikes so quickly, that Roberta doesn't have time to react. He wraps the wire around her neck and applies pressure. Roberta struggles to pull the wire away from her neck to keep from being strangled. She tries to scream, but only gagging sounds come out of her throat.

Acmen watches Tufa killing Roberta and he laughs glee-fully.

THE FIRST LADY

Roberta stops struggling. Tufa feels her body going limp. Suddenly, the door to the patio-pool swings open and a happy Lovel comes in briskly. He has an ice bucket with the champagne bottle in it and two glasses.

Lovel is stunned when he sees what is happening. He drops the champagne and glasses and they fall on the grass area of the patio-pool. Like a raging bull Lovel comes to Roberta's aid. He leaps on Tufa who is forced to release his grip on Roberta to defend himself. Acmen races to help Tufa. When he gets into the melee Lovel is surprised that Tufa has a partner.

The three men are in combat. Lovel fights like hell, handling himself pretty good. He throws punch after punch into the faces of the two intruders.

When Roberta catches her breath, she recognizes the two assailants. She knows Tufa and Acmen are Sheik Seid's men and that he must have sent them to kill her and Jasmine. She gets to her feet and jumps into the fray. She punches them, kicks them, slaps them all to no avail. So then she wraps both of her arms around Acmen's neck and tries to pull him away from Lovel, but she can't budge him. Then a thought hits her. She swiftly, grabs Acmen by his testicles and squeezes them with all her might.

Acmen screams in agony, trying to pull Roberta's hands away from his private parts, but no go. He struggles with Roberta, but she holds on to his balls for dear life.

With a vise-like grip on his organs, Roberta starts pulling Acmen to the edge of the pools deep end. He tries to resist, he can do nothing but comply to her wishes. Roberta sees that Acmen is a little off balance as she lets go of her grip on him, she pushes him into the pool.

Acmen, immediately sinks to the bottom of the pool like a lead penny. His head hits the surface finally and he begins spitting out the water he has swallowed. Acmen tries to stay afloat, but can't.

It is obvious to Roberta that Acmen can't swim and she doesn't give a damn.

"Tufa, help me." Acmen cries. "I am drowning, someone help me." screams Acmen.

Tufa wants to help him, but he can't, he is trying to save his own life.

Again, Acmen sinks to the bottom of the pool and again he comes back up to the surface of the water. Then he drops down to the bottom of the pool for the third and last time. Acmen has drowned.

Tufa is now alone as he fights to get away from Lovel. But he can't. Lovel holds on to him and keeps punching him. Then Tufa, throws a lucky punch at Lovel that lands on the side of his head almost knocking the governor out. Tufa keeps punching Lovel trying to render him unconscious.

Roberta sees that Lovel is in trouble. She picks up the bottle of champagne, raises the bottle over Tufa's head and with all of her strength she hits him square on the back of the head. Tufa falls like a big tree.

Roberta helps the groggy Lovel to his feet. "You okay, Raymond?" says Roberta very concerned.

"I'm Just a little woozy. I'll be alright," says Lovel as he wipes the blood from one of his eyes. Lovel sees that Roberta's neck is badly bruised. "Do you feel alright, Roberta?" asks Lovel also very concerned.

Roberta touches her neck and winces a little. "I'm just a little sore. I'll be okay. But I don't think he will," says Roberta as she points to Acmen's body that is now floating face down in the center of the pool.

"I think we better get off our feet," says Lovel as he takes Roberta's arm and guides her to a bench. They both sit.

"Raymond, you saved my life. Thank God you came in when you did. I would have been dead for sure," says Roberta with moist eyes. She puts her arms around Lovel's neck and places her head against his chest.

"Everything is going to be alright now. I won't let anybody hurt you," says Lovel gently smoothing out Roberta's hair.

Roberta, likes Lovel's tenderness and manly concern for her. Lovel looks lovingly into Roberta's face. "Roberta you are beautiful and

THE FIRST LADY

I care for you very much," says Lovel raising her chin and kissing her on the lips.

"I feel the same about you, Raymond. I never felt this way about, any man," says Roberta smiling and again leaning her head on Lovel's chest.

"Roberta, what's been puzzling me is why they were trying to kill you?" asks Lovel.

"I don't know. I really, don't know. Maybe they took me for someone else," says Roberta convincingly.

"Well, let me wake that guy up and find out what he has to say," says Lovel firmly.

"Oh, yes, that's a good idea," says Roberta hiding her apprehension.

Lovel goes to Tufa's body that is lying face down. He rolls Tufa's body onto his back and tries to revive him, but it is of no use, Tufa, is also dead. "Well, he's dead too," Lovel reports.

"I'm sorry he was hitting you so hard, I had to do something," says Roberta who deep inside of her was relieved. But she also was upset by the deaths of Tufa and Acmen. She starts to cry.

"Hey, don't feel sorry for that bastard. He and that other guy tried to kill you and me," says Lovel trying to comfort Roberta.

"But, we will never know who they were." Roberta still crying and exhausted, is saying to herself, over and over, "Thank God. Thank God. No one will ever know about Roberta."

Lovel breaks out in nervous laughter while explaining, "With all the ruckus that was going on out here nobody inside heard anything."

"Yes, let's go tell them what happened. They will be shocked and surprised," says Roberta still shaken.

WILLIAM HELLINGER

Lovel takes Roberta in his arms and kisses her. Roberta is about to push him away, but instead presses her lips tightly against his. Roberta is in love.

Chapter Twenty-Three
The Sheik Abdicates

The afternoon sun's hot rays reflected on Sheik Seid's Palace. In the Palace study Sheik Seid and Doctor Kalila are sitting in chairs watching an American Newscaster on television that is coming via his satellite dish from the United States.

"And from all reports that I hear, movie critics, who were at a screening last night of 'The Perfect Woman,' say that Roberta Mann's performance is so sensational that she will become Hollywood's new number one female star. And at the same screening her press agent announced that she and Governor Raymond Lovel of South Dakota, flew to Mexico and got married," reports the newscaster with a happy smile. Then a picture of Roberta and Governor Raymond Lovel flashes on the television screen and stays there for a moment. Then the newscaster comes back on.

"There is talk that Lovel's party is going to nominate him as their Presidential candidate in the up coming convention in San Diego. If he is elected we'll have another actress for a first lady. A beautiful one too. Good luck, Roberta," says the reporter.

The Sheik angrily presses the remote control button to turn off the TV set. "That dirty lousy, son-of-a-bitch bastard. I created a monster Rashid. I still can not understand how Tufa and Acmen got themselves killed. They were good men, my best men! May Allah Damn her." screams the angry Sheik in English while banging the top of his desk with his fists. The Sheik begins to pace the floor and he stops when a thought comes to him. "Roberta and Jasmine will die. Rashid, I should have thought about this before. If I had, Tufa and Acmen would still be alive," says the Sheik in English with an ominous smile.

"Ali what are you thinking?" asks the doctor in Arabic. "Rashid, do not speak our native tongue. The walls have ears. Speak in English," says Seid in English. The doctor nods 'yes' to the Sheik's request.

"Good, Rashid I have a contact in Rome who can get me MAFIA hit-men in America to do the job for me and I will pay them five million dollars to make Roberta and Jasmine disappear," says Seid with a crazy laugh.

"Ali, you are brilliant, they never miss," says Rashid joining the Sheik in laughter.

Their laughter is so loud that it is hard for them to hear the phone on the desk ringing. Then after six rings the doctor hears the telephone ringing. Rashid quickly picks up the cellular phone and gives it to the Sheik.

"Yes, oh, Rasafi, yes," says Ali quietly, humbly in Arabic as he moves to his desk chair. "Yes." The cellular phone is glued to his right ear as he listens intently to Rasafi on the other end of the line. Doctor Kalila observes Ali on the phone and gets very concerned. He sees beads of sweat rolling down Seid's tense pale face.

"Yes Rasafi, I will. Thank you my dear friend. May Allah be with you and give you long life," says the Sheik in Arabic who face reflects distress and worry.

"Ali, who is Rasafi and what is wrong," asks the concerned doctor

"Rasafi is King Jamal's personal secretary and my child-hood friend. He warned me that the King's advisers have just gotten the proof from the Prime Minister that I am skimming money from Bokuf's oil profits. The Minister got into my secret bank account in Curacao. King Jamal has ordered the head of the army to send a squad of soldiers to arrest me and take over my Palace and property," says the miserable Sheik.

"Oh, Ali, what will you do?" asks the very concerned doctor.

"Get the hell out of this country. I did not think that they would ever find out. Rashid, I thank Allah for preparing me for this event," says the Sheik as he heads for the study door.

"Ali, wait. I will go with you. I will not stay here without you," says Rashid with urgency in his voice.

"My dear Rashid, I did not ask you to go with me because I did not think you would want to join a runaway thief of a Sheik," says the Sheik opening the study door.

"Ali, you are my good friend and it was you that made me the head doctor of your Palace when I graduated medical school," says Rashid gratefully.

"Good, I want you come with me Rashid. I do not want to be alone, you were always a good friend to me and I will take care of you very well. I have a case full of American dollars enough to take care of us for a while. When that money is gone I have a secret savings account and a large safe deposit box full of bonds and cash in a U.S. bank," confesses the Sheik who is now anxious to get the hell out of his Palace.

"Oh, that is wonderful Ali. You will not be sorry you took me with you," says Kalila thankfully as he joins the Sheik at the study door.

"Rashid, there is another reason why you should get away from here. When the soldiers see that I have escaped they will question you to try to find out where I have gone. If you tell them you know nothing, which will be true. They will torture you to death to find out," says the wily knowledgeable Sheik.

The Doctor Kalila nods his head to the Sheik in agreement and the two men exit swiftly out the study door.

Chapter Twenty-Four
The Escape

Some time later outside of the Sheik Seid's Palace the late afternoon sun begins to set. Its shadows reflect rays on the large front gates of the Palace.

The gates suddenly swing open and a red Suburban Ford shoots out to the road that leads to the highway, leaving a trail of dust behind it. When the red vehicle gets to the main highway it moves swiftly.

Sheik Seid's back is pressed against the corner of the seat in the red Suburban car. His face is pale, tense and worried. He hugs an alligator leather attache case very tightly. Doctor Kalila is sitting next to him with a look of concern and expectation.

Kariff his personal chauffeur is driving with his foot pressed down on the gas pedal. Kariff had looked into his rear view mirror for an instant and was very concerned when he sees that his Sheik and Doctor Kalila have looks of apprehension on their faces. He then looks away from them and focuses his eyes on to the road ahead of him while presses his foot further down on the gas pedal and the car soars foward.

"Ali, did Rasafi tell you who betrayed your Curacao bank account information to the Prime Minister?" asks the inquisitive doctor.

"He told me it was my Harem. Ayesha was the leader of them, she was in charge of all my business dealing. I trusted her. She is the one who suggested that I hide the money that I took in a secret Curacao bank account. I agreed and she set it up," says the Sheik with bitterness.

"But, all your wives loved you, especially Ayesha. She was the most loyal of your wives. Why would they do this to you," says the surprised doctor.

"Rasafi said that they really hated me and wanted to be free. So then they could follow the professional educations I gave them. It is all my fault. If I had not let them watch all those trashy movies and soap opera's from the United States, they would not have seen all those free and independent American women. I was too good to them, I should have whipped all of them." screams the Sheik.

"Yes, you should have. They were not grateful," agrees the doctor as he gives a sympathy pat on Seid's shoulder.

"Kariff, head for the Saudi border," says the Sheik in Arabic with a new energy.

"Ali, why not take your jet," says the doctor not thinking.

"No. The airport would be the first place that the Prime Minister would send Army patrols looking for me and everywhere else," says the experienced Sheik.

The sun drops like a basketball behind the deserts horizon. The Sheik's red Ford barrels down the dark highway, its bright headlights picks up a sharp bend in the road. The Ford slows down its speed and moves slowly around the bend and disappears into the darkness of the night.

Now its early morning, the desert sun is bright and hot. Its rays hit the Sheik's red Suburban as it speeds down a two lane desert road.

The car flashes past a sign on the side of the road that reads, '100 Kilometers to the Saudi Arabian Border'. As the car travels down this road an Oasis becomes visible on the horizon.

The red Ford picks up speed. Its tires churn up the road dust, as it closes up the distance to the desert Oasis, when suddenly, vapors of white steam bellow out of its overheated engine.

THE FIRST LADY

An Oasis is a place that God made for travelers and wayfarers of the vast desert. Occupying this Oasis is a Bedouin tribe with its camels and goats. Sleeping tents are scattered around the area. Fires with pots of boiling meats are cooking. Tribesman and their woman are doing their chores. The tribes children are playing, some swimming in the large pool of cool water.

Karem is leaning against a tall healthy palm tree near the edge of the shore watching the kids. Then he closes his eyes. His face reflects happiness and serenity as he begins to think of how great it is to be away from the mad, sadistic, revengeful Sheik Seid. "How wonderful Allah is for helping him find his uncle's Bedouin tribe, also for his uncle's acceptance of him and Abdullah who are now part of the tribe." Karem is overjoyed with his freedom, "He wishes that he could shout this to the heavens He tilts his head up, opens his eyes and looks up to the beautiful morning sky that bleeds through the luscious leaves and branches of the palm tree. Karem is so happy to be alive and free that it makes him sigh with contentment.

Abdullah is carrying a young tribe boy on his big shoulders. when he approaches, his friend Karem, Abdullah says in Arabic with a happy smile, "Good morning, Karem."

"Yes, Abdullah, it is a very beautiful morning," says Karem smilingly.

Abdullah takes a deep breath and looks around the Oasis. He could not hide how he felt. He looks at the boy and laughs. Then he shouts in Arabic, "I am alive, I am free." He still continues his laughter as he runs around the palm tree several times. The boy on his shoulder laughs with him. He finally stops, th en lifts the young boy off his shoulders and places him on the ground.

"Thank you for the ride, Abdullah," says the little boy in Arabic as he runs into the water to join the other kids who are enjoying themselves.

"Karem, this Bedouin life is good, out in the open air, under the desert stars, free. I love it. Thank you my friend for bringing me here," says the happy Abdullah as he sits down next to Karem.

WILLIAM HELLINGER

Karem smiles in agreement to Abdullah's sentiment. But just as Karem is about to say something to Abdullah there is a sound of a car motor sputtering. The two big men get up on their feet and look in the direction of where the sound comes from. They see the red Suburban Ford. The car looks very familiar to them. It is coming into the Oasis with swirling heavy vapors of steam coming out of its radiator. When the car comes to a quick halt, Karem and Abdullah look at each other in puzzlement. The heavy screen of steam coming from the engine of the car makes it very difficult to look through the car's windshield to see who is in the car. The Ford's hood pops up. Kariff gets out of the vehicle and lifts the hood open. When Karem and Abdullah see that Kariff is the driver they are now certain that red Suburban Ford is Sheik Seid's car. They have seen this car in the Palace garage amongst all his other cars. Karem and Abdullah look at each other quizzically.

The tribesmen begin gathering around the stalled car.

"Abdullah what in Allah's name is Kariff doing all the way out here," declares Karem.

"I do not know, so let us find out," says Abdullah. He and Karem start towards Kariff.

When Karem and Abdullah get closer to the red Ford they see Sheik Seid and Doctor Kalila get out of the back seat of the car, their mouths drop open. They are very surprised and happy to see this Devil and this advocate doctor in their territory in big trouble.

"Abdullah, Allah is good and very powerful. He has brought this evil man here to pay for his terrible sins," says Karem with justice and ironic faith in his voice.

Abdullah smiles, nods his head in agreement. "Wait until your uncle Habib finds out who he is," says Abdullah with a happy laugh.

Sheik Seid and Doctor Kalila are stunned when they see Karem and Abdullah coming toward them with ironic smiles on their faces. The Sheik and Kalila go white with fear. Karem and Abdullah grab Seid firmly with ironic smiles that turn to looks of revenge.

THE FIRST LADY

"Ah, my Sheik, it is so good to see you," says Karem touching the long scar on his face.

"Karem, Abdullah, I have money. Please let me go," begs the frightened Sheik.

A full moon is shinning over the desert and a blanket of bright stars dot the black sky behind it. The Bedouin tribe are on camels with all their belongings. They are moving out of the Oasis into the cool desert.

Karem and Abdullah are on horses and each one of the horses have a rope that is tied to a Donkey's neck harness. And mounted and bound to each Donkey with rope, is Sheik Seid and Doctor Kalila. Their faces reflect fear and hopelessness.

Karem and Abdullah turn to their captives and gives them a big, "now we got you" grins.

The Bedouin herd of goats and other animals follow close behind the two new permanent additions to the tribe, a pig's ass of a Sheik and his doctor that assisted the French surgeon who turned Robert Anthony. into a woman. A life of servitude is a fitting sentence for these two men.

Later that night the red Suburban Ford makes its way down a desert road with its bright headlights piercing the dark road ahead it. Kariff is behind the wheel. He isn't wearing his chauffeur clothes but clothes given to him by the Bedouins. He is happily singing the last strains an old Arab love song. His happy thoughts are of Karem and Abdullah. They helped him plug up the leak on the red Ford's radiator and then let him go free. They gave him plenty of water for the road. They advised him "Do not go back to the Sheik's Palace. If you do go back, you will be arrested and grilled for Seid's where-abouts and then thrown into jail for complicity, for only Allah knows how long."

Kariff laughs. He thinks how things turned out for Sheik Seid. He never liked Sheik Seid for the way he treated him and all the people who served him at the Palace. They were his slaves. As the Sheik's chauffeur he always remembered how the Sheik talked to people on his car phone. He was cruel, mean selfish and threatening to them and also a pompous ass, the bastard got what he deserved.

WILLIAM HELLINGER

The headlights pick up a sign on the shoulder of the road that reads, 'Saudi Arabian border 25 kilometers'. When Kariff sees that sign he begins to smile broadly. He extends his right hand inside the Sheik's open attach6 case that is on the seat next to him. As Kariff begins to finger the stacks of American p1000 bills he starts singing the Marseillaise, the French March of Freedom.

The Suburban Ford's, headlights paves the way down the dark desert road. The car picks up its speed and moves further down the deserted road. The rear end with its red lights disappears into the darkness. Sheik Seid's red Suburban Ford and his money, are taking Kariff to a comfortable life in Saudi Arabia or where-ever else he wants to go.

Chapter Twenty-Five
Mr. & Mrs. Candidate

A large happy crowd of people are in front of the San Diego Convention Center where 'Banners declare that the Independent Party' is holding its convention to nominate a Presidential candidate in the coming election.

The city police are trying to keep the noisy crowd in order as they move back and forth in front of the convention building. The eager people hold up campaign posters with Lovel's picture on them and chant loudly, "LOVEL FOR PRESIDENT. "LOVEL FOR PRESIDENT." They continue chanting, "LOVEL FOR PRESIDENT." They are drowning out other people who are trying to speak out about their favorite candidates.

The convention hall is filled with happy, noisy Independent Party delegates that came from every state in America. Banners and posters of different Presidential candidates are held up by repre-sentatives of the fifty states through-out the massive hall. Party Chairwoman Sally Chambers is standing behind the podium waiting patiently for the ballots to be counted, to see who will be the Independents Party's candidate to run for President of the United States.

The noisy delegates begin to yell, "The boys in the back room are taking their time counting the ballots!" The delegates continue their complaint until a man, a party delegate, comes out from the stage wings carrying a large brown envelope. He gives the audience a big smile, moves to the podium, and hands the envelope to Party Chairwoman Chambers.

WILLIAM HELLINGER

The noisy hall becomes silent. All of the faces of the delegates show anticipation. Chairwoman Chambers thought that she would milk this very important moment. Savor it, let everyone in the hall stew. She gives the audience a big smile, takes her time in opening the big brown envelope, you can hear, clearing of throats and mumbling of inaudible invectives.

Finally Chairwoman Chambers takes out the sheet of paper, looks at the name of the candidate. Now the room gets noisy again. With a big smile she picks up her gavel and raps it on the podium several times to silence the delegates. The hall becomes silent immediately.

"The third ballot has been counted and it is unanimous. Our party's candidate for President of the United States is Governor Raymond M. Lovel." shouts the smiling Chambers into the podium microphone.

The entire hall goes wild. They scream for Lovel to come out to the podium. Lovel comes out from behind the curtains holding Roberta's hand. With winning smiles on their faces Roberta and Lovel move close to the podium and when they do the room becomes as silent as a church.

"My wife Roberta and I, thank you all for this great honor, that, you have bestowed on me. I won't disappoint you, we will win," declares Lovel with a victorious smile into the microphone.

The entire delegation goes wild, chanting Lovel's and Roberta's name.

Roberta and Lovel are extremely happy, they smile broadly and raise their clasped hands in victory.

Chapter Twenty-Six
A First Lady At Last

Roberta, Lovel, Jasmine, Aunt Bea and the Governor's campaign manager Barney Stoneridge with staff, are in Lovel's large palatial living room of the Governor's mansion in South Dakota. They are all seated in chairs facing a 60 inch TV screen. The remote TV cameras are picking it up on New York City Streets and Broadway. It is election night and they can see how heavy the traffic is. The crowds of people are milling about the area with their eyes fixed on the news buildings neon crawl waiting for a Presidential news up-date.

Everyone in the room is waiting with anticipation for that important news up—date.

Roberta is sitting next to her husband sipping a glass of wine. Her eyes are fixed on the TV screen, then she turns her look towards her husband. She sees that his eyes are bloodshot and tired and she is very concerned.

Roberta begins thinking how she met and married Raymond Lovel. She was amazed how very much she could really love a man, this man, so good, so honest.

Lovel notices Roberta is staring at him. He gives her a big smile and an encouraging look. She knows that he is trying to cover up the way he really feels. He is tense, scared and unsure of himself.

WILLIAM HELLINGER

Roberta did know that the most important thing in Raymond Lovel's entire life was to become the President of the United States. So he could give the country back to the people by running America the way our forefather's intended it to be run.

Roberta's head shifts back to the TV screen. She hears a CBS male newscaster's voice with a election up-date and sees him with his female co-anchor in the Network press room. There are garbled voices of men and women in the background working on computers to get election reports from all over the country.

Every eye in the large palatial room is glued to the big screen.

"So far it has been a close race, with Brown the incumbent slightly ahead of Lovel!" reports the Newscaster.

"Yes, Tom, but that could change. The precincts in all the States aren't in yet.

Barney Stoneridge jumps in quickly. "It's not over yet Ray, we can still pull this off!" says the campaign manager with encouragement. Lovel smiles while nodding his head.

Roberta puts her hand into her husband's hand. "Honey, you will be the next President of the United States. I know it. I can feel it," says Roberta somewhat like a sooth-sayer.

"From your lips to those casting the electoral votes," says Lovel hiding his apprehension with a smile. He kisses Roberta on her cheek.

Suddenly there are loud bursts of screams and whoopies that come from the people in the C. B. S. TV news room. Lovel and Roberta focus their eyes on the big tube. A young male reporter, with a broad smile, hands the Newscaster a sheet of paper with an up-date election report that just came in.

The newscaster scans the report. "Leslie, the electoral votes from the Western States are all in and they put Governor Lovel over the top. Brown has conceded the race, making Raymond M. Lovel the next President of the United States of America," reports the excited Newscaster.

Everyone in the large room shouts with joy as the Newscaster continues his report. "Most of the electoral votes came from the North Western States and," says the happy Newscaster.

Barney Stoneridge, Lovel's press manager turns the TV set off. Roberta has wrapped her arms around her husband's waist and everyone in the room has gathered around them. "Congratulations, Mister President. We knew you could do it."

Jasmine and Aunt Bea take Roberta aside. Everyone on Lovel's staff surrounds him, giving him advice and asking him questions.

"Roberta, I can't believe it! You are the first lady. I'm so proud of you," Aunt Bea is crying with happiness.

"Especially Sheik Seid, when he finds out it is you, he will have a stroke," Jasmine says laughing.

"I hope so," says Roberta seriously.

"Of course you know, he will never admit to who you are. He could go to prison for the rest of his life," says Jasmine knowingly.

Roberta is about to say something to Jasmine when Lovel comes to her, "Honey, you're not only my fist lady, but the President's fortune teller," Lovel kisses Roberta hard on the lips.

Barney Stoneridge, pops open a bottle of champagne and pours some into each glass. "Alright, let's toast the new President of the United States and his First Lady. May you both live in the White House for eight years and have many children while you're there," declares Barney downing his drink.

Lovel laughs and smiles to Roberta. Roberta just giggles and says to Barney, "And if the first one's a boy, we'll name him Barney."

Every one in the room laughs, even Aunt Bea, until she begins to think. She stops laughing. Jasmine wants to laugh, but instead smiles, looks over to Roberta and then tilts her head skyward.

WILLIAM HELLINGER

The bleachers are filled with invited guests along with U.S. Congressmen and Senators. Sitting in the front row seats proudly smiling are Jasmine and Aunt Bea. Joe and Ellen Canin, Diana and Harry Stuart are sitting behind them in the second row. They are all present to attend Raymond Lovel's Presidential Inauguration in Washington D.C.

They are all observing Supreme Court Justice Rose Monte, dressed in her black robes, giving the oath of office to Lovel. He has his right hand raised. Standing along side of him is his beautiful, red haired, happy smiling First Lady, Roberta Mann.

"And will to the best of my ability, protect and defend the Constitution of the United States," Lovel is repeating what Supreme Court Justice Monte has just told him to say.

Lovel lowers his hand and the crowd applauds the smiling new President and his First Lady.

Chapter Twenty-Seven
A Night to Remember

Two years have gone by quickly in Washington DC for President Lovel and Roberta his First Lady. They both have been extremely happy with each other living in the White House. Since his election, Lovel has changed things in America. His polices have given the United States a great economy and peace around the world. Roberta stood by him and encouraged him in every political decision her husband, the president had to make. The opposing political parties favored his changes and the American people have great trust in him and love the First Lady, Roberta. There has been talk of his re-election possibilities, and if that happens, Roberta will wait four more years to resume her film career in Hollywood.

Aunt Bea with Sam live in the White House too, she works for Roberta arranging parties in the White House for VIP'S and foreign dignitaries. She loves her work and being close to her niece Roberta.

In those two years Jasmine has come into her own. She has created a successful Sexology business with a list of Hollywood clients and many other people and some very influential individuals seeking her help. Roberta has made sure that Jasmine is a frequent visitor at the White House. She stays in the Lincoln room and she loves America and being with Roberta.

Up to now, everything for Roberta has gone great, except for one thing, she fears that her husband might find out who she used to be and if that happens her life is over. Every day she thinks about telling Raymond her secret, even if it destroys her.

It is early evening in the Presidential bedroom of the White House and President Lovel is lying on the bed in his robe with his back resting on a pillow that is propped up against the headboard of the bed. He is going over proposed congressional bills making notes on a pad, regarding the bills that are before him.

Roberta comes out of the bathroom wearing a see-thru negligee that reveals her beautiful body.

Lovel stops what he is doing when he sees her come into the room. "Sweetheart, you get more beautiful every day."

"Thank you, darling, you're very sweet," says Roberta with a big sensual smile. She moves to the bed and sits down at the edge of it. She leans over to him, kisses him on the cheek, smiles and mouths 'I love you.' Lovel smiles back and mouths 'me too' and goes back to work. Roberta stares at her husband for a moment. Her face registers a decision. "Honey, have you been happy with me?" Roberta starts softly.

"Of course, I love you," responds Lovel smiling.

"I love you, very much. That's why I have to tell you something you have to know," states the determined Roberta.

Lovel smiles and puts the papers aside, pulls Roberta close to him. "That serious, huh," says Lovel jesting.

"Yes, do you remember when Barney made the wish for us to have many children while you are President?" Roberta is now shaking. "Of course I do," says Lovel with a little laugh.

"Well, for me to have children would be impossible," says Roberta quickly turning her head away from her husband.

"Honey, that's all right," Lovel says as he is very calmly kissing her on the forehead.

"It doesn't bother you?" says Roberta very surprised.

"No, not unless it bothers you," says Lovel with a loving smile.

"Well, no, I." Roberta's guts start to burn.

"Honey, I just hope you're okay." Lovel hugs Roberta.

"Oh Raymond, I can't continue this game any longer. I love you too much. I must confess to you why I can't have babies," cries out Roberta. "I must be honest."

"All right, tell me, but just take it easy," says Lovel with a big smile.

Roberta gets off the bed and stands there holding her breath.

"Well, it all started when this Arab Sheik kidnaped me," says Roberta taking another deep breath.

Lovel's brows furrow giving Roberta a very puzzled look. "And when I woke up eight months later," Roberta who is now feeling so guilty for waiting this long to tell him ,turns her back to him. She can not look into his eyes, as she reveals her harrowing tale of Robert Anthony, his murder, the birth of Roberta Anthony and the transformation. When Roberta gets through with her confession she begins to weep softly.

Lovel is now in shock and he responds, "Oh, my God." to Roberta's hellish story. Lovel becomes silent and deep inside of he feels betrayed, confused and angry. Anguish comes over him as he stares at Roberta for a long moment then closes his eyes tightly, afraid that he may cry. After a moment he opens eyes, gets to his feet and quickly goes out of the bedroom leaving the door ajar.

Roberta turns to the bedroom door, "Oh, Raymond, oh Raymond." cries Roberta. She falls on to the bed and her cries turn to a wail.

Lovel quickly goes down the White House hallway passing doors that lead to other rooms. He reaches a door at the end of the passageway.

He stands there for a moment, then knocks on the door twice and after a moment, "Yes," says a female voice.

"It's Raymond, Aunt Bea," Says Lovel somberly.

"Oh, one moment Mister President," says Aunt Bea respect-fully. After a moment the door opens and Lovel is greeted by Sam. Lovel pats Sam on the head as he says, " Aunt Bea, I must speak with you."

"Of course, of course, come in. You too, Sam," says Aunt Bea knowingly. Lovel goes into the room, closing the door behind him.

Roberta is lying on the bed on her side, crying very softly. After a while she turns on her back and the tears from her eyes flow down her face. Roberta takes hold of the bed sheet, wipes her eyes and face and begins to sniffle. She rolls to the edge of the bed and sits there for a few moments. Then she gets to her feet and goes into the bathroom. She stares at her face in the bathroom mirror and sees that her eyes are red and swollen from her crying and pain. She turns the cold water on in the sink and starts to bath her eyes and face many times trying to relieve the burning sensation from her eyes. She finishes washing her face and takes hold of a towel from the towel rack and begins drying her eyes and face very gently.

Sam suddenly comes into the bathroom and Roberta is unaware because her face and eyes are buried in the towel drying them. Sam paws Roberta's thigh and a makes soft bark to let her know that he is there. She quickly pulls the towel from her face, drops it to the floor and gets on her knees and hugs and kisses Sam. Sam starts licking her face and she hugs him tighter. "Oh, Sam, Sam baby. How did you get away from Aunt Bea?" says Roberta now with a little smile on her lips.

"I did sweetheart," responds Lovel who's voice is coming from the bedroom.

Roberta is taken by surprise and she quickly gets to her feet and goes out of the bathroom with Sam following her.

Tearfully, Roberta rushes to her husbands waiting arms and they kiss, look into each others eyes lovingly and tenderly. He guides her to the bed and sit close to each other at the edge with his arms around her waist.

THE FIRST LADY

"I talked with Aunt Bea. She told me you wanted to tell me who you were before we got married," reports Lovel. Roberta nods her head.

"And she told you not to," continues Lovel.

"Yes," responds Roberta truthfully. "I wanted to tell you but I couldn't," Roberta mumbles.

"You were against her opinion and wishes, but finally she convinced you to be silent," says Lovel with a loving smile.

"Yes, but as time went by I couldn't continue to live with this lie, because I loved you. That's why you had to know," confesses Roberta as tears come to her eyes.

"Please sweetheart, don't cry," begs Lovel holding Roberta tightly in his arms. "I forgive your silence. I now understand." a soft smile comes to his handsome face. "My love, I don't care what you were then, but only what you are now. You're my beautiful, loyal, caring wife and I love you very, very much," he pauses and then hugs Roberta very tenderly. "My love, if we ever want any children we can always adopt." He strokes Roberta's face.

Roberta throws her arms around his neck tightly. She smiles as tears of joy start to roll down her tear stained face.

"Sweetheart maybe we could adopt a little girl," says Lovel as he wipes away Roberta's tears with his finger.

"Oh, yes, my darling and possibly a little boy too," Roberta suggests.

Lovel smiles and nods his head.

"And we can name him, Robert Anthony," says Roberta with contentment.

"Of course my sweet, anything you want," Lovel kisses his First Lady on both cheeks and her lips with tender love.

WILLIAM HELLINGER

Sam has been lying nearby watching the two lovers and when they start to make love, he gets to his feet and goes into the living room. He closes the living room door with his paws and lays in front of it guarding his mistress the First Lady and the President of the United States her husband.

THE END

About The Author

William Hellinger Author - publisher started his career as an Actor in New York on Broadway films, television, a regular on the Phil Silvers show. In Hollywood he was in the New York company of Three Penny Opera. After Three Penny closed he stayed in Hollywood and appeared in television films and series. At that time he became interested in writing. His first story sale was "The Fugitive" which got him a membership in the Writers Guild Of America West. He was under contract to Universal Pictures. and wrote some of their TV shows, Laredo, Name Of The Game, Ironside, etc. He wrote produced and directed a short, "The Cycle" that played in movie houses and was submitted for an Academy Award. He was one of William Castles writers after "Rose Mary's Baby." Now in Las Vegas he Produced and wrote a Film titled "Rock-A-By Terror. Currently involved in a Film project to be produced in Mexico.

Printed in Great Britain
by Amazon